IMPERFECT STRANGERS

by D.V. Nobles

D.V. Nobles

iii

D.V. Nobles

CHAPTER ONE

There was no warning. The sound of screeching tires punctuated by the scraping of metal against metal interrupted the quiet surroundings. Jack, who had been sitting quietly at the dining table and blowing smoke rings, got up slowly and walked to the large window in the living room. He pulled the curtain aside and peered out at the front drive. A small, gray sports car was wedged nicely under the rear of his blue pick-up. The driver got out and quickly ran to the front of the vehicle to survey the damage. She wore big, dark glasses. Her long, auburn hair was brushed back behind her shoulders. She took quick, short steps around the car to view it from the other side. With hands on her hips, she bent down and peered underneath the pickup as if looking for a lost pet. Finding nothing, she hurried back around and jumped into the driver's seat. With a generous amount of acceleration, the car shot backward and screeched to a quick stop. The shiny hood of the car now bore several long scrapes upon its surface. Jack shook his head and walked back to the dining room table and sat down.

After a moment of silence, the front door flew open. The woman charged in with a large bag under one arm and an oversized purse swinging haphazardly from the other. She paused just inside the door and kicked it closed with one of her spiked heels. Her short, red skirt revealed a pair of long legs, darkened by pantyhose. The tight skirt and the heels seemed to be the culprits behind her quick, small steps. Lifting her sunglasses just above the eyes, she spied Jack's cigarette smoke drifting from the dining room.

"Hello? Is that your truck out there?" Her voice whined in a high-pitched nasal tone. "I can't believe this. My poor car is ruined. Would you take a look out there? Would you look at the damage?"

She was making her way to the dining room when suddenly her purse caught on an end table and the contents spilled out all over the floor. Several containers of makeup, a couple of prescription bottles and a cellular phone eventually came to rest. "Lovely," she said. She put her bag down on the floor and began scraping the mess back into her purse. "Hello? Would you take a look at my car, please?"

Jack emerged from the dining room and looked down at the new arrival. "It's a tough old pickup. I've had it for years, I'm sure it's alright."

"Pickup?" She stretched her arm across the floor to retrieve wayward lipstick while looking up at him incredulously. "I'm not talking about the pickup. I want you to look at my car. The hood is ruined."

"Probably is," Jack said. "What do you want me to do about it?"

She gathered the rest of her belongings and stood up to face him. She had to look up to him. Not only was he quite a bit taller than her five foot six, but the living room was a step lower than the rest of the house.

She said, "What I want you to do is give me an idea of how much it will cost to repair. I'm not going to have you charged with anything, I just want --"

"Wait a minute," Jack cut her off, "you want *me* to pay for the damages to your car because *you* ran into the back of my truck?"

She plopped her purse onto the nearby end table with a thud. "Well, if you had pulled up all the way and didn't have the tail end of your truck sticking out, I never would have hit it."

Jack looked at her in total disbelief and patted his chest pocket, looking for another cigarette. He said, "You've got to be kidding, lady. Okay, let me tell you what: Why don't I go out there and see how much damage I can total up on my truck that *you* need to pay for?"

She seemed to ignore his words completely. "All I know," she said, ripping her purse from the table, "is that somebody is going to pay for the damage." She looked around as if noticing the interior of the house for the first time. She said, "Where's all the other people?"

Jack lit his cigarette. "We're the only ones here so far," he said.

She looked back at the living room and noticed the staircase. She marched up the stairs and disappeared from view. A moment later she bent down from the top of the stairs. "Where the hell's the bathroom in this place, anyway?"

***

The silver BMW cruised gently around the mountain's curves at a relative speed of 56 miles per hour. John Forest sat in good posture as he took in the view and handled the steering wheel with a single index finger. "You know, dear," he explained, "these people we are going to live with could be any kind of people. They could be crooks or murderers for all we know."

"Thank you, John, that's such a comforting thought," his wife, Gail said. She was reclined in the passenger seat with a blue gel pack over her eyes. An infomercial had sold her on the idea that the gel pack inhibited wrinkles. She wore it every chance she got. "The only reason I agreed to this fiasco," she continued, "is because you thought you might meet some financial prospects. If you had taken the time to actually read the letter, you would have seen that these people come from 'varied backgrounds'. Like you said, they could be anybody. But no, you just assumed that they would all have money."

Her husband rolled his eyes. "I know, I know. Well, look at it this way: We don't have anything else to do and they are paying us for this little vacation. When have we ever been paid to take a vacation?"

She lifted up the gel pack and eyed him for a moment and said, "You think this is going to be a vacation?"

***

Jack investigated the refrigerator. It appeared to be well stocked. He reached his hand in-between the milk and orange juice and combed through peaches, applesauce, some kind of lunch meat and small bottles of cranberry juice. Damn, no beer.

As he closed the door, a faint sputtering could be heard in the distance. At first, he thought someone was running a lawnmower somewhere. He knew that was absurd, though, as the house was almost completely isolated in the mountains. Then, as he listened, the sound grew louder and more familiar. Someone was pulling up in a VW beetle. He walked over to the window above the sink. Slightly ahead of a dust cloud from the dirt road, a puke-green vehicle that sounded like it wasn't running on all cylinders made its way up the hill towards the house. As it slowed to a halt, the tailpipe belched a couple of loud backfires before the engine died. A thin, young man got out and scratched his curly hair. He looked up at the house, squinting in the sunlight. His expression was one of perpetual sourness like he had been sucking on lemons.

Jack was startled from the view by a loud crashing noise towards the rear of the house. He quickly made his way down the hall where he stopped just short of the back door. The door itself was open and intact, but the deadbolt housing in the frame was completely destroyed. Standing just outside the entrance was the most physically fit woman Jack had ever seen. She wore black combat boots bloused over by camouflaged fatigues. A small, black belt facilitated a number of objects around her waist. The short-sleeved army green T-shirt that clung to her toned body was slightly soaked with sweat. Her face was quite remarkable, boasting high cheekbones and a brazen color. Her piercing black eyes matched the color of her hair, which was cut butch, marine style. She stood there like an impenetrable obstacle, her muscular arms ready at her side. Upon seeing Jack, a quick flash of surprise came into her eyes, but it was masked immediately by a menacing look of curiosity.

Jack widened his eyes expectantly. He said, "Can I help you?"

She gave a quick, single nod to indicate the entire house. "You live here?" A hint of Hispanic origin was in her voice.

"I do this week," Jack replied. "Along with whoever else shows up. I guess you're one of the chosen few, eh? Look, just because I was the first one here, people seem to think I know what's going on. I don't. So why don't you come in, make yourself at home and…try not to break anything else."

"So, this is…the meeting place," she said tentatively.

"Yeah," Jack said, "unless you're looking for the rest of your troops."

"Humorous."

Jack started back towards the hall, but turned and gestured towards the back door. He said, "You know, you could've knocked or at least used the front door. It's not locked."

She glanced at the damage without really seeming to consider it. "The damage is minimal," she said. "It can be fixed." Then she strode quickly past him.

Back in the living room, there was a small rapping on the front door. It was a persistent, barely audible noise. The army woman went to the kitchen and began opening cabinets and examining their contents. As Jack walked to the front door, he called out to her. "See? This is not so hard. You give a knock on the door," he reached for the handle to open it, "and someone on the other side comes to let you in."

The face of the kid from the VW bug met him. This close-up, he could see several curly strands of hair dangling out from under his chin. It was nothing that could be classified as a goatee, but more than would be caused by lack of shaving. For some reason, it instantly irritated Jack.

"Hello, my name is Gerald." The young newcomer smiled a lemon sour smile. "Is this the experiment house?" He squinted up at Jack like he needed glasses.

"You found it," Jack said. "Come on in."

Gerald walked in like a cautious mouse expecting the cat at any moment. Looking around, he said in a humble, nervous voice, "Wow, this place is nice. Like a vacation home in the mountains or something."

Jack went back to the kitchen, balanced his cigarette on an ashtray and casually watched the army woman snoop meticulously through the cabinets. "Looking for something in particular?" he asked her.

She turned quickly around to face him and said, "What is your name?"

"Name's Jack."

"Well, okay, 'Jack'. Am I bothering you?"

"No, I was just wondering what--"

"No? Good. So, will you do me a favor? Don't talk to me. Don't ask me any questions, don't try to make conversation. In fact, don't even look at me."

Jack picked up his cigarette and watched her as she continued into the cabinets. "Fine by me," he said.

High-heels tapped across the hardwood on the second floor before descending the stairs. "I can't believe this! There are only five bedrooms up here and there's supposed to be six of us. Someone's going to have to sleep on the couch." She stopped suddenly at the foot of the stairs, lowered her sunglasses and stared at the newcomer in the living room.

"Hello, my name is Gerald," he said, moving his arms to different positions, trying to settle upon a relaxed appearance. Unable to obtain this, and growing more nervous from her stare, he quickly sat down in the closest chair.

She started again, like a mannequin coming to life and walked quickly to him with an outstretched hand. "Hello, Gerald. My name is Heather. Heather DuMorrier." He shook her hand vigorously and gave her a tight, thin smile. She withdrew her hand and looked over it as if inspecting for tiny damages caused by the experience. "Do you know anything about the costs of car damages, Gerald?"

Jack, who had been taking in the scene from the kitchen entrance, rolled his eyes and turned back to the army woman. She appeared to be almost finished with her cabinet inspection. She opened the last one on the bottom row and peered into the darkness. Suddenly, with a hiss and a gnarlin' sound, something jumped out at her and dug its claws into her shirt. She jumped back in surprise, tumbling to the floor. There were a few seconds of confusion as a gray and white ball of fur trampled over her. She wrestled with the creature, adding to its distress and causing sharp claws to dig deep. For a moment, there was a mixture of screeching, grunting and swearing. The cat suddenly pounced from the intruder and took off down the hall towards the back door.

In a fit of rage, the army woman jumped to her feet, simultaneously pulling a knife from her belt and flung it towards the cat's last known position. It struck smartly into the back door just as the cat disappeared through the opening. She grunted angrily, ran down the hall and quickly retrieved her knife. Looking beyond the open door and into the yard, her jaw became set and her face stern. Revenge filled her eyes.

Jack raised an eyebrow at her and turned to see Gerald and Heather rushing into the kitchen area. "What on earth is going on in here?" Heather demanded. "Who is that?"

"I don't know who she is," Jack said, crushing out a cigarette, "she broke in through the back door and now she's at war with the resident house cat."

Gerald wrinkled his nose. "She broke in?"

The army woman came back towards the kitchen and

stopped. She looked down, examining the bleeding scratches on her arms. Sensing a stinging pain, she moved the back of her hand up to touch her face. When she lowered it, there was a small streak of blood on it. Then she looked up at them through fierce eyes, still holding the knife as if ready for an attack. "Listen to me, you morons," she said, speaking through her teeth and moving closer to them, "I don't know who you are or where you're from. I don't want to know and I don't care. But stay the hell away from me. You stay out of my way and I'll stay out of yours."

Gerald was shaking visibly, watching the knife in her hand. Heather was aghast, her face wearing a combination of surprise and disgust. Jack retrieved his pack of cigarettes and tapped them a few times, forcing one to expose itself. He pulled it out and wedged it between his lips, a smirk forming on his face. "That's a pretty nasty scratch on your cheek," he said. "I'd say the cat won."

The army woman turned to him, her eyes narrowing momentarily before she spun on her heel and headed for the back yard.

Gerald let out a fluttering breath. "You don't really think she's going to kill that cat, do you?"

"Who cares about the cat?" Heather said, "What you really have to worry about is that we have to sleep in the same house with that psycho."

CHAPTER TWO

Paul looked around at the surrounding wilderness, a gritty smile spread over his face. Out here, in the middle of nowhere, he felt at home.

He possessed some kind of connection to the outdoors that he couldn't define. It was the basic need to be at one with nature that beckoned him from the small town where he lived. It called him away unexpectedly, not unlike the silent call that birds hear to fly south for the winter. But it wasn't winter, nor was it an annual call. When he felt the urge, he just went, with no regard to any responsibilities that might hold him back.

He liked working on cars. He was good at it. Working at his brother's garage in town gave him ample opportunity to exercise his mechanical talents, but at the end of the day, it was just plain hard work.

Being outdoors was different. He felt a higher purpose in the woods. The harmony of everything living in the wild filled his soul with a kind of elation he could experience nowhere else. The sights, sounds and smells of the great outdoors were his inner peace. Out here, his mind seemed clearer, more focused. He could be at one with nature.

Paul leveled the barrel of his rifle on the old dead tree next to him and squinted, lining up the sites. He focused his gaze beyond the gun sites, spying a wild rabbit in the distance. The animal was innocently chewing on some vegetation, completely oblivious to its fate. A mischievous grin crept across Paul's face. Tonight's dinner was going to be delicious.

Another car pulled up in the driveway. Once parked, the engine purred softly for a few seconds before it died. Heather dashed to the kitchen window to get a glimpse of the newcomers. Two people emerged from a silver BMW. The driver, a well-groomed man in his early fifties, stretched as if preparing for a golf swing and looked up at the house. Then, he actually did take a swing, as if he was using an invisible golf club. He put his hand to his brow, watching his invisible shot disappear into the far distance. His wife, not yet immediately visible, was loading luggage over her shoulders like a trained caddie. She came around to the front of the car and loaded her husband up with a few bags. The two of them stood there as if they were contemplating whether they actually wanted to go in or not. From Jacks position at the table, he could see them. He estimated at least middle-upper class. They stood there for a moment and then moved towards the front door.

Heather let the window curtain wave back into position. "Well, that explains the lack of bedrooms. They're married. That's good because there's no way I'm going to sleep on that couch. Not only does it look uncomfortable, but that trashy yellow color, ugh!"

Gerald opened the door for them. The older man stared at him for a second, not certain that he had found the right place. After a few seconds, he nodded politely and he and his wife walked in with a number of bags, mostly golf equipment. They piled it up into a nice heap in the middle of the living room floor and the man thrust out a steady hand to Gerald. "John Forest." He said and smiled genuinely as the grip caused Gerald's hand to make strange little crackling noises. "This is my wife, Gail."

"Nice to meet you guys. My name's Gerald and well, these are the other people that will be living here." He waved a twitching hand towards the kitchen where Heather was descending from the single step that separated the two areas.

"Heather. Heather DuMorrier." She smiled, her eyes sparkling with over-politeness as she almost curtsied during the introduction. She greeted John and his wife with an obligatory smile and stepped to one side as the two made their way towards Jack.

Jack made the effort to reach across the table to Mr. Forest's hand. "Jack Eastman. Nice to meet you."

After a firm handshake, John Forest clasped his hands together as if about to announce a main event and said, "Well, we'd better go and get the rest of our bags. If someone would be kind enough to show us to our rooms, we'll move our things out of the living room."

Gerald gesticulated nervously. "Oh, I don't think it matters what room you get. I think they're all pretty much the same."

Heather came to life once more, her posture almost humble and her voice the epitome of politeness. "Excuse me, Mr. Forest, but did you say 'rooms'? I may have misunderstood you, but it did sound as if there was a tiny little 's' on the end of that word."

"Why, yes. I did say 'rooms'. You see, my wife and I do not share the same bedroom."

Gerald's hand crawled spastically about his neck in embarrassment and Heather's mouth opened slightly as if she were going to say something and then stopped. Jack propped an arm up on the table and wedged it between the surface and his chin, not wanting to miss this for the world.

Mr. Forest looked at the expressions for a second. "Oh! No, you do not understand. It is not that my wife and I are not in love or do not share the physical pleasures thereof. We have simply reached a point in our relationship in which we respect each other's individual time alone. Being financially independent, we share almost all of our time together. One thing that we definitely enjoy is sleep, as I am sure most of you do, and we use the separate rooms as sort of a 'rest' from each other. Well, I'm sure you understand."

The others nodded slowly in polite, awkward understanding. Heather raised her hand slightly as if she were asking a question in a school classroom. "Um...Mr. Forest?"

"Please, call me John, dear. If we're all going to be living together for a week, we might as well be on a first name basis."

"Of course, John," Heather continued, "we understand. The only thing is...well, there are only five bedrooms here and there are six of us. It would make more sense for the two of you to share a room than for say, me and..." She looked at Gerald for a split second and then waved her hand behind her. "...Jack or somebody. You understand."

John clenched his jaw a little. "There appears to be only five people here," he said. "I don't see what the problem is."

"There's another woman here," Gerald said. "She's...kind of weird."

John turned halfway in his direction and demanded, "Well, where is she now?"

"She's out in the back attempting to kill the house cat," Jack offered.

John looked confused. Then his wife, Gail, moved closer to him and put an arm around him. "It's quite alright, dear. After all, we haven't actually slept in the same room for a long time. It'll be different. Like a *vacation*."

They gathered their belongings and hauled them upstairs. John appeared to be very stiff as he walked. It was almost as if he were in a state of subdued shock.

CHAPTER THREE

The nighttime somehow brought a greater sense of seclusion to the already remote location of the house. Jack's cigarette lighter glowed momentarily in the dusky surroundings of the outside deck. He shielded the fire from the gentle breeze that brought in the night air. The large wooden deck was just another luxury the house afforded. A few benches lined the edges of the railings and an octagonal picnic table was nicely situated off to one corner. It was to this table that Jack had taken retreat a few hours earlier. Now, as the first beginnings of darkness started to descend from the distant hills, more of the others came out to relax.

John Forest lit a pipe and stood at the railing, gazing out over what he could see of the back yard and the hills. His wife, Gail, slumped down one of the benches. She looked tired from her trip. Gerald was out in the yard close to where the trees began to thicken. He kept cupping his hands into a circle around his mouth and calling, 'here, kitty, kitty, kitty'.

"I wouldn't mind owning some land up here," John said, cradling his pipe in one hand. "I wonder if there's any for sale."

Heather emerged from the back door. When she pulled the door to, the brass handle came off in her hand and she stared at it and said, "Um…this is not my fault."

13

"No," Jack agreed, "the army woman did it when she broke in. I'm sure she'll fix it."

"Sure she will." Heather took quick little steps and sat down at the table across from Jack. "Do you know what she's doing in there? She's going through the entire house. Searching closets, drawers and everything else she can get into. I'm telling you, that woman is not playing with a full deck. I wouldn't doubt it if she goes through the attic next."

"She is quite odd," Gail said, "and I'm not going near her. She's made it clear that she doesn't want her space invaded."

Gerald walked up the steps onto the deck. "I know the kitty's out there somewhere. I could hear it moving around in the bushes. She must have really scared it to death." He took a nearby seat and propped his head up on the railing, squinting out at the darkness.

John took a seat at the table. "So, Jack, what is this all about? Do you know?"

"I guess I know as much as all of you. I got a letter in the mail. I thought it was junk mail and I almost threw it away. It was a few paragraphs talking about an 'experimental social gathering'. It said I would be paid ten thousand dollars to spend a week living with a few other people. That's when my interest started to perk up."

"What I can't understand," Gail said, "is what kind of experiment is being conducted. We're supposed to live with each other for a week. We can't leave the area for any reason unless it's a medical emergency. I mean, what's the big deal? We don't even have anyone to report to on how things went. It doesn't make any sense."

"Well I know what I'm going to do with my money," Gerald said, still staring into the woods. "I'm gonna fix up my bug. A new paint job and some engine work and I'll be ready to cruise the beach."

"Gerald, why don't you use it to put a down payment on a *real* car?" Heather said.

"It is a real car." Gerald squinted at her, his voice bending in defense. Then he grinned. "It's a classic."

"If you don't mind my saying," Jack said in John's direction, studying the end of his cigarette, "you and your wife seem to be pretty well off. Why would you agree to this gathering?"

John cleared his throat. "You are quite correct, Jack. We are not hurting for money, that's for certain," he said, as Gail turned back to the yard again, "but I found it quite an intriguing opportunity. You see, I am a businessman and in good time, I'll have a financial proposition for each and every one of you. Besides, my wife and I have been working day in, day out lately. I thought it would be a good idea to get away from it all."

"This is definitely away from it all," Heather said in disgust. "The nearest town is thirty miles away and there's not a phone or television in the house. Have you noticed that? And my cell phone doesn't have any signal here, either."

"Well, I guess that was the idea," Jack said. "To live up here isolated from everything else. It looks like we have enough food to last over a month, let alone a week. The cellar is packed full. But I do agree with Gail. This 'experiment' doesn't make any sense. I'm no intellectual by any stretch of the word, but I've always thought to have an experiment, you have to observe and record the results."

"That's it!" Gerald stuck a finger into the air. "Record the results. Maybe they're watching us right now. Maybe they have hidden cameras all over the place and watching our every move." He walked down the wooden steps and started examining the outskirts of the deck.

"Oh, please," Heather said inwardly. "Paranoid delusional."

"That may not be far from the truth," John agreed.

"You honestly think there are cameras all over the place watching us?" Heather asked, astounded.

"No," John explained with a whisper, "paranoid delusional." He smiled at her, his eyes darting back to where Gerald was now examining the wall of the house where the roof began.

15

Heather smiled back, her own eyes sparkling in the dim light.

Gail suddenly tiptoed to the table and whispered, "Hey, there's something out there."

Heather looked up at her. "Gail, the man is strange. Don't let it get to you."

"No, I'm serious. Listen."

They all became quiet as Gerald prodded around. But there was another sound. A rustling noise seemed to be coming from the nearby woods. Jack broke the silence. "It could be anything. A deer. A bear. The killer housecat."

"There are bears here?" Heather whispered incredulously.

"There's a lot of different wildlife up here in the mountains," Jack explained. "Don't bother them and they usually won't bother you."

Heather looked around in the direction of the woods, seeing nothing but darkness now. "I'm going back inside now and getting ready for bed. I guess I'll see you all in the morning."

John smiled. "Good night, Heather DuMorrier." Gail looked at him, her eyes narrowing as Heather's shoes clip-clopped back into the house.

Jack stuffed a pack of cigarettes in his shirt pocket. "To answer your question, John, I don't have the foggiest idea what this is all about. As long as they send me the check as promised in a week, I really don't care. I suggest we all take it as a vacation. It's sort of like being at a bed and breakfast."

"Yes, of course," John said. "It's only a week. What could happen in a week?"

***

Heather lay in a state of half sleep. This was a strange house and, like any other unfamiliar place, she had trouble getting to sleep. She tried to make herself relax. She told herself to ignore the unfamiliarity and imagine she was in her comfortable apartment back home in the city. It was not easy. There were sounds outside that she never had to deal with. Instead of the occasional car horn, ambulance and rush of traffic, there were the constant sounds of crickets or some other insect. These were interrupted at times by the hoot of an owl or the sad call of a night bird. There were other sounds that she could not identify but knew that they must be a natural part of the great outdoors. At least she hoped that's all they were. These sounds irritated her and she finally had to resort to the one thing she knew that would comfort her: Mr. Wiggly. Mr. Wiggly was a plush, stuffed pink pig that she retained from her childhood. She didn't sleep with Mr. Wiggly all the time but reserved his calming powers only for emergencies such as these.

She was well on her way to sleep when she was startled by a couple of definite 'thumping' noises. Her eyes snapped open and she looked up to the ceiling. She held her breath and lay unmoving, waiting to hear the sound again. *Maybe it was my imagination*, she thought. No. There it was again. It was a definite sound of movement. She listened intently. It was something very big. *Too big to be a rat*, she thought. This brought her both relief and alarm as her mind raced with possibilities.

Then, realization flooded her thoughts. She clenched her teeth and was suddenly angry with herself for not knowing sooner. Angry for letting her heart skip a beat in fear. Angry at this absurdity at one o'clock in the morning. Her arms tensed, holding Mr. Wiggly tightly against her chest as she rolled over and buried her head between two pillows.

The army woman had found the attic.

CHAPTER FOUR

Gerald made his way cautiously down the stairs. He was wrapped in a thick blanket, which his concealed hands held onto tightly. His eyes, usually nothing more than squinting slits at best, did not appear to be visible. A wonderful breakfast aroma managed to awaken him from a peaceful sleep. It was about eight in the morning. Gerald never got up at eight in the morning. Maybe nine or ten, but never earlier. He was too sleepy to ask himself what he was doing out of bed.

Following the scent of food, he walked into the large dining room adjacent to the kitchen and was instantly blinded by sharp rays of morning light. Someone thought it would be a good idea to part the curtains from the great window at the other end of the dining room. Not in agreement with this thinking, but recovering from the light, he began to notice the others in the room. John Forest sat on one side with his wife. He had a day-old newspaper spread wide open and appeared to be studying it behind dark-rimmed glasses. Gail appeared to be straightening her silverware. Heather sat on the opposite side of the table, staring at the other side of John's creased newspaper. A nice helping of bacon, eggs and toast sat on her plate, but she seemed to be politely waiting for the others to receive their serving before she started. She turned and looked at Gerald, her eyebrows twisting and one end of her upper lip slightly curving. It was her personal expression, containing a mixture of disgust and disbelief while at the same time projecting a sort of indifference.

Gerald walked around the table and settled into the seat next to hers. His face maintained its sleepy, zombie-like appearance. He stayed like that, clutching the blanket around him and waiting for his brain to wake up. Then, the kitchen's doors swung open and Jack appeared with a plate in each hand. He wore a white cook's apron that read 'master chef at work'. It seemed odd that this man who, for the most part, conveyed a macho tough-guy image could actually cook.

"Wow," Gerald said, "Jack of all trades."

Jack stopped in mid-delivery and stared at him. Gerald kicked his mind into gear, realizing what he said. "Oh!" He laughed slightly. "I didn't mean for it to come out like that. I mean, Jack being your name and all."

"How do you like your eggs, Gerald?"

"Oh, whatever's easiest. Over- easy is...er...fine."

Jack stared at him again and then disappeared into the kitchen. Gerald turned to Heather. "I really don't mean to be smart or anything. My brain isn't due to wake up for another hour or so."

"Gerald, why are you wearing a blanket at the breakfast table," she asked him flatly.

He looked down at the untraditional accoutrements. "I'm just so cold when I get up in the morning. This is really very comfortable."

Heather looked down her nose at him. "It's very rude is what it is."

"Well, it would be," Gail interjected, "if this were a formal restaurant. I certainly hope you won't object if I decide to come down in my nightgown at some point."

"I guess I'm just used to adhering to my strong sense of manners," Heather said, perking her nose in the air.

Soon, Jack appeared with two more plates. He sat one down in front of Gerald with his over-easy eggs and placed his own collection of scrambled eggs at the head of the table. John folded up the newspaper as well as his glasses and soon a clinking of silverware could be heard. Sounds of food appreciation emanated from everyone except Heather. She seemed to be picking through her eggs as if inspecting for microorganisms and avoided her bacon like it was nuclear waste.

"Where's our military expert this morning?" Jack asked.

"Probably in the attic," Heather said with a cutting malice in her voice.

"That can't possibly be what I heard last night," Gail said incredulously.

"I'm afraid so," Jack said. "Could I have the salt, please?"

John stopped for a second. "What on earth does that young lady hope to accomplish by personally acquainting herself with every nook and cranny in this estate?"

Gerald gulped down some food. He said, "She really needs to get some psychiatric help."

"Boy, isn't that the truth," Heather agreed.

"Oh, come on now," Gail protested, "we don't even know her. I admit, she seems a little, uh, different, but give her a chance. I don't think we should be making these wild accusations. Especially if she's not here to defend herself."

"We'd rather she didn't defend herself in our presence, dear," John said. "The last time she did, she nearly murdered the cat from what I understand."

"Has anyone seen the kitty yet?" Gerald inquired suddenly.

"I really don't think you will ever see the cat again, Gerald," John said in an empathetic, yet matter-of-fact tone.

Jack had been eyeing Heather as she finally finished the last of her eggs. The strips of bacon were neatly piled in a stack off to one side. "Didn't like the bacon, Heather?"

"My nutritionist told me that you should only have one strip of bacon. It's very unhealthy to eat any more than that."

"You haven't even eaten one," Gail remarked.

"One strip of bacon *per year*," Heather clarified. "I've already had my bacon this year."

Gerald squinted at her. "I'll eat yours if you don't want it."

She promptly slid the plate in his direction. John chuckled in amusement.

"Well, there are six of us," Jack stated. "I figure I can do all the cooking today. If each of us cooks one day each, that will leave the last day. We can draw for it or something."

"I don't cook," Heather said.

"What do you mean you don't cook?" Jack asked, slightly irritated.

"Which of those three words did you not understand, Jack? I. Don't. Cook."

"What do you eat?" Gail wondered aloud.

"I eat out. Either someone makes it for me or it's something that can be eaten as is. I have no desire to cook or to learn to do so. Is that clear enough for everyone?"

Jack shook his head in disbelief. "A woman who doesn't cook."

Heather glared at him. "That's just the kind of chauvinistic statement I would expect from you, Jack."

"Well," Gerald began, "I can cook a little. I don't know if anyone will like it, but I'll do my best."

"Thank you, Gerald," Jack said and turned again to Heather. "At least he's willing to try. I'll bet that our military friend isn't going to help us out either. That means four of us will have to cover the week. The ones who don't cook," he directed his statement to Heather, "will just have to help out in other ways."

There was a loud pounding at the front door. They all glanced at each other in slight bewilderment before John arose. "I'll get it," he said.

Just before John made it to the door, the pounding repeated. This time it was louder and more insistent. He opened the door, already wearing his ready-made smile and prepared to give his best greeting. Once his eyes took in the vision before him, however, his smile disappeared and the greeting did not come out as it was originally intended. "My word," he said.

A large bear of a man stared back at him. His entire body was extremely hairy, with the bulk of the follicle growth concentrated around his big, round face. Underneath his tattered jacket, he wore a dark green shirt that strained to confine his ample belly. The baggy jeans he wore were also in ill repair, being faded and full of holes. What really startled John the most, however, was the fact that the man was clutching a rifle in one hand.

"Well howdy to you, too," the man said. "This the place?"

John attempted to regain his composure, trying to stop his quick glances at the firearm. "The uh...place?"

"Yeah, man, you know. The experimental place or whatever."

"Oh. Uh, yes. You...you're one of the...uh, one of us?"

"Yeah, that's right," the larger man said. You gonna invite me in or what?"

"Oh, I'm sorry. Where are my manners? Yes, please come right in."

By now, the others had gathered in the living room out of curiosity. Heather, completely appalled by the man's appearance, managed to make the astute observation: "I thought there was only supposed to be six of us."

"That's what I thought, too," Gerald said.

"Muh names Paul," he introduced himself, "but people call me polecat."

The others introduced themselves while also taking notice of the gun. He received a grimacing smile from Heather, a polite acknowledgment from Gerald and Gail and a firm if unreadable handshake from Jack.

Going completely unnoticed, the army woman descended the stairs. She paused long enough to allow scrutinizing eyes to look over the newcomer and his weapon. Her dark eyes filled with angry suspicion before she disappeared again.

Jack looked briefly around at the others before speaking to the man. "Paul--"

"Polecat."

"Uh, Polecat," Jack said carefully, "we were all under the impression that there would only be six of us staying here."

"Well," Paul let out a chuckle, "unless I done forgot how to figure, there's only six of us here."

"There's another woman here," Gail explained. "She pretty much keeps to herself."

"Oh. Well, all I know is I got some letter that said I'd get me ten thousand bucks if I came up here and lived for a week with some other people. I wasn't about to turn down that kind of money."

"I see," John said and spoke to the others. "Well, he's definitely...one of us. The only problem is that there aren't any more bedrooms."

Paul held up his hand. "Not a problem," he said. "That couch right there looks mighty comfortable."

"Well, we can't ask you to do that," John protested. "It wouldn't be fair to you. Perhaps we could all take turns on the couch."

"I am not sleeping on that couch," Heather stated flatly.

"I've got back problems," Gerald complained. "I need a good, solid bed."

"Dear," Gail began, "how are we going to take turns? We would both have to sleep on the couch. Unless you're planning on sharing a bed with Pa-- uh, Polecat." She was met with a scowling glare from her husband.

Paul put up his hand again to ward off the problem. "Look, people, I've slept in some of the worst rat-holes there is. This couch don't bother me one bit. That's that. Problem solved."

"Well, if it doesn't bother you..." John said.

"Not a bit," he said and, as if to prove it, walked over sat down quickly. The cushions sank and conformed to his large body.

Jack stood with his hands tucked in his pockets. "Do you always carry that gun around with you?"

"What? Oh, this thing? I like hunting a lot. Don't worry, it's not loaded. Never bring a loaded gun in the

23

house, muh paw used to say."

"We didn't even hear you drive up," Heather said. "Did you walk here?"

"Well, actually, uh what's your name again, ma'am? Heather! Actually, Heather, I'm kinda familiar with the area. I drove up around the hills a few miles away. I thought I could get some hunting in before I showed up. A little bit after sunrise, I headed this way. I can walk for miles. It don't bother me."

"You left your vehicle out in the woods?" John asked.

"Yeah, it's hidden pretty good. Not many people around this area anyways. And lemme tell you, if somebody does steal it, they'd be doing me a big favor." He laughed.

"I'm surprised they let you join us this late," Jack said. "They were very clear in emphasizing that we had to live here together for an entire week."

"Yeah. Well, they wanted me to let all of you know that I was sort of an exception. I guess they wanted one more person, I don't know."

"I guess so," Jack concluded.

"Well, I hate to barge right in and start eating, but I'm starving. What kind of food yall got in this place?"

"There's some stuff in the refrigerator and piles of food in the basement," Gerald offered. "Come on, I'll show you."

Once they were out of sight, Heather converged on the others, lowering her voice to a quick hiss. "I don't like this one bit. The letters we all received said there would only be six people. Not one more, not one less. Now, all of the sudden, this guy appears out of nowhere and a day late. It doesn't make any sense."

Gail responded with an empathizing tone. "Now, there's no reason to doubt this man, even though he does seem a bit...'rough'. We're all here from varied backgrounds."

"You mean to say," Heather corrected, "that we're not all rich."

Gail was taken aback. "I meant nothing of the sort."

"Oh, but I think you did," Heather said, her voice still in its low hiss as if the new arrival was within earshot. "You've had that condescending attitude since you and your husband got here. Well, let me tell you something, dear, you're not the only one here that's accustomed to high living standards."

Gail's eyes widened as if attacked with the worst of insults. "I don't know where you're getting your attitude from, but you don't want to cross me, sweetheart, I'll..."

"Please, please...ladies," John said, putting his hands on his wife's shoulders to calm her down, "there is no need for this hostility. For goodness sake, we haven't even gotten to know one another yet."

"I think I know more than enough," Heather said. She spun on her heels and stormed up the staircase.

"Yes," Gail yelled up after her, "that's your problem."

Jack, who had watched the whole thing with a sort of disinterested amusement, walked towards the kitchen to make some more coffee.

CHAPTER FIVE

Heather sat quietly in the living room recliner, inspecting her fingernails. Gerald sat on the sofa, his knees pinched together with his long arms resting over them. John and Gail sat next to him, patiently waiting to hear why they were there. Paul stood up against the fireplace mantel, inspecting the crevices within the stonework of the fireplace.

"Can't you at least tell us what this is all about, Jack?" Gail asked.

Jack was slowly pacing the living room floor. Every once and a while, he glanced at his watch. "It'll be clear soon enough..."

As if on cue, there was a sound at the back door and then footsteps sounded in the hallway. Jack quickly moved towards the staircase as the army woman approached. He ran up a few steps and took hold of both sides of the banister, making an obstacle out of himself. She stopped quickly and looked at him, her eyes a menacing glare.

"We're having a little meeting here. I'd appreciate it if you would join us."

"I don't participate in 'meetings'," she said, coldly. "Move out of my way."

"I would rather you participate in this one. Especially since you are the subject."

The army woman looked calmly over to the group in the

living room. When she saw Paul, their eyes met in a quick glance of mutual distrust. They were all staring at her. Then she turned back slowly and faced Jack, her dark eyes sinister and narrow. "What you people do is your business," she said, her jaw tightening. "Don't include me."

"I'm afraid you're already included," Jack said carefully, "I really think you should join us for a group discussion."

"And I really think you had better move out of my way."

"Go into the living room and take a seat," Jack slowly demanded.

For a split second, her eyes narrowed even more. Then, she quickly lunged at Jack, taking hold of his right arm. She would use his elevation to her advantage. He was heavy, but it didn't matter. All she needed to do was to gather a little momentum towards her shoulder. Then, she would heave him over easily. It was a good maneuver. One she had used dozens of times. Usually, the unwilling victim was one of those macho men who figured they could take what they wanted. Others were unworthy opponents who either underestimated her or proclaimed they would not fight a woman. Fools.

She pulled his arm and turned to complete the maneuver. But something went wrong. When she was at the point of heaving Jack over her shoulder, she suddenly couldn't move. His hand had a firm grip on her lower pant leg. Before she knew what was happening, Jack twisted her arm back around and pulled it up the middle of her back. He pulled it up until he could feel her muscles stiffen, holding it there while she winced again, this time in pain.

"Now," he said, "would you be so kind to join us?"

He let go of her arm and she pulled away in anger, glaring at him as she moved into the living room. "You'll regret you ever did that," she said, relinquishing herself to a nearby chair.

"Well, Jack," Paul said enthusiastically, "you managed to get us all in one place at the same time...even commando woman. This must be pretty durn important."

"I'll get right to it," Jack started. "I went back up to my

room a little while after breakfast. All my belongings had been gone through. Everything. And I'm willing to bet that it's the same story with everybody else's stuff."

"What?" Heather leaned forward in the chair. "Who would do such a thing?"

"Jack, I just came from my room not long ago," John said. "Everything seemed to be in order."

"Oh, it's not noticeable," Jack explained. "Everything in my room was almost exactly as I left it."

"Then how do you know?" Gerald asked.

"Because I know. What I don't know, however," he turned to the army woman, "is why."

"You can't prove I did anything," she protested angrily.

"Can't I? Shall we resort to DNA testing?" He held up a single strand of straight, black hair pinched between his fingers. It matched hers. "I found this in my room. You've been combing this house inside and out since you got here. Just what have you been looking for?"

"You went through our personal belongings?" Gail asked, incredulously.

"You could have asked," Gerald said, meekly. "I don't have much, but I would have let you look through it if you had a good reason."

"Ugh! I don't believe this," Heather stood up. "You have no right whatsoever to go barging through other people's things."

"I think you owe us an explanation, young lady," John said.

The army woman leaned forward in her chair. "Didn't any of you morons ask why they wanted a group of total strangers to live together in the same house for exactly one week? Sure, the ten thousand dollars is yours, but only with a 'no questions asked' tag attached to it. This whole thing reeks of some type of government experiment. You want to know what I've been doing? I've been looking for bugs. I've been looking for hidden surveillance equipment. It strikes me as very odd that none of you are the least bit concerned that our right to privacy is being infringed upon.

For all we know, they're using us as guinea pigs."

"We're all concerned about why we're here," Jack said evenly, "but I think you're completely paranoid. As for a government experiment, you're the only one wearing fatigues around here. But I agree with you that our privacy is in danger what with you going through our stuff. I can't speak for the rest of us, but if I ever find you've been in my room again, it'll be the last time you invade my privacy."

The army woman was glaring at Jack. She was obviously doing all she could to restrain herself, appearing as if she would spring from the chair and attack at any second.

"I think it would suffice," John said, "if you would offer us all a polite apology and ensure that you will not again trespass and...rummage through our personal things."

"An apology?" The army woman looked around at them in complete amazement. "I was doing all of you morons a favor. Granted, I needed to know for my own self, but you all would have benefited if I found anything."

"I don't think we need you looking out for us," Jack told her. "Besides, according to you, we've already got 'big brother' doing that."

"I'll tell you what I think," she hissed. "I think one of you is a spy. I didn't find one microphone, one camera. So how else will they get any results from whatever experiment they're doing? And from what I understand," she turned to Jack, her eyes suddenly full of enlightenment, "you were already here before anybody else."

Jack looked around the room to see everyone suddenly looking at him, awaiting a response. He rolled his eyes. "I can't believe this. You're not going to turn this around on me. If I were a spy, wouldn't it make more sense for me to come here after a few of the others so I wouldn't arouse suspicion like this?"

"Good return, Jack. Sounds well rehearsed," Heather said, nonchalantly.

"This woman is combative and paranoid," Jack said, pointing an accusing finger at the army woman. "If you want to side with her, that's fine, but I'd keep a close watch on my things if I were you."

Paul let out a slow, high-pitched chuckle. "Man, you people are somethin' else. All in a tizzy over somethin' like this."

Heather turned on him quickly. "That's easy for you to say, Mr. Polecat, you don't have any belongings with you. What if she started messing around with that...that gun of yours?"

Paul held out a chubby palm. "Look, did she steal anything? Did she muss up anything? You done did what you needed to. You told her not to do it again or else. She does it again, kick 'er out of the place. She don't do it, then no harm done. Ain't no need in sittin' around here griping about it. Give it a rest."

Gerald winced. "Um...we can't really kick anyone out. If anybody leaves here, that voids our agreement. No one will get any money."

"Yeah, that is a good point," Paul mused.

The army woman suddenly stood up again. "I've told you all before. I don't care who you are or where you come from. Stay out of my way and I'll stay out of yours."

"Just make sure you stay out of my stuff," Jack said coldly.

She looked at him again momentarily, her eyes foreshadowing vengeance before she stormed out the front door.

CHAPTER SIX

John Forest had his attaché case open on the dining room table. A number of papers were sprawled out from where he was sitting at the head of the table to the chair next to him where Paul was firmly seated, his ample body testing the chair's endurance. He hunched over a particular sheet of paper that John had given him, studying the contents. His eyes scanned over a paper that was lying on top of the rest. John had a large landscape sheet in front of him that bore a survey of a property.

"...and I'll tell you something else," John was saying, "this property is more valuable now than ever before. There's an airport nearby. If they expand it, and I know they will, the value of this land will shoot through the roof."

Paul let the paper dangle between two fingers. "Yer saying that I could double muh money?"

"At the very least," John insisted, stabbing an index finger at the property map. "You know property...it always goes up. Actually, chances are you could triple your investment. I mean, think of it, Polecat...here you are with ten thousand dollars that you didn't really expect to have. Sure, you could take that money and have a big party, invite a few friends over and before you know it, Wham! It's the next morning and you don't have anything to show for it. Believe me, I know. Ten thousand dollars just doesn't go very far these days. It's spending money. But if you invest it, now that's a different story. Instead of having a quick ten grand now, you could have twice that later. It's the smart thing to do."

Paul eyed the paper again. "Yeah?"

"Yes, it's practically a guaranteed high return investment. Do you know anyone in real estate that's poor?"

Paul chuckled in realization. "No, they all dress fancy and drive nice cars."

"That's right! Look at me. See the way I dress? See what kind of car I have? Believe me, I wasn't always this well off. I had to work my way to the top and I tell you, it was no easy road. I had to scrape and claw for every cent I could get until I got into real estate. Then, there was the matter of learning the rules of the road. You see, real estate has its own special set of hurdles to overcome. But once you learn the secrets, you have it made. Now, I don't want anyone to have to go through everything I did to get to where I am. There is a lot of work and headache involved. Why should you have to go through all that when I can help you?"

Paul squinted, eyeing John suspiciously. "Why would you want to help me?"

"It's simple. I like to see others succeed. There's no point in others having to work as hard as I did to get to where I am now. There is plenty to go around in this business. If I can come back later and see how well off you've become just because I helped a little, then that would be job satisfaction in my book. It makes me feel like a better man if I've helped a fellow human being up the ladder of success. Besides, don't feel like I'm not getting anything financially out of this. I get a small percentage if you buy the land, but that's all I get. The money doesn't matter to me at all when I compare it to your success. I really want you to succeed."

"Well, it sure don't seem like a bad deal," Paul said. "Twenty acres of land for ten grand ain't bad at all."

Jack was standing at the other end of the table, his hand wrapped around a mug of coffee. His face held little expression, but he listened intently to the conversation, occasionally glancing out of the window. Gerald could be heard from time to time, calling 'here, kitty, kitty, kitty' from somewhere outside.

Finally, Paul stood up, stretched and yawned. "It sounds good to me, Mr. Forest. It sounds real good. You gotta let me think on it some, though. I don't want to say for definite right now 'cause I haven't really thought much about what I'm gonna do with the money."

"Oh, of course," John said, standing up also, "I'm not going to rush you into anything. You think about it as much as you need to. Just let me know by the end of the week because these deals don't last very long when I find them."

***

Outside, Gail walked up to Gerald, who had just let out his loudest, most frustrated 'meow' yet. "I take it you're a cat lover, Gerald?" she asked.

"Oh, yes. I've always liked them, ever since I was little. Cats are the least offensive of creatures, you know. Unless they're provoked or something. That crazy military woman scared the poor thing away. Maybe forever."

"Well, you may be right, Gerald. I mean, about that woman. She doesn't seem to be on the same wavelength as the rest of us."

Gerald laughed nervously. "Boy, that's the truth. Who in their right mind attacks a poor defenseless animal with a knife? I wish I had known the cat was in the cabinet, I would have taken it somewhere safe before she found it."

Gail hesitated before speaking again. "Gerald...I think you may have to consider the fact that she actually found it and killed it, dear."

Gerald shook his head violently. "No. Oh, no, I'm not going to believe that. Cats are smart. They can hide in places we could never find or even think to look in. I know it's out here somewhere. I'll find it. I think this is its home and it's just afraid to come back because she's here."

Gail sighed and gazed out at the wondrous tree line that decorated the mountainside.

***

"Oh, but John, what in the world would I do with twenty acres of land?" Heather objected politely.

"That's the beauty of it, my dear. You don't have to do anything with it. Just let it sit there if you like."

"Let it sit there," Heather giggled girlishly. "Well, what good would that be?"

John smiled. "Just imagine...you have this nice piece of property sitting all by its lonesome somewhere. Meanwhile, the real estate world goes on. Property prices rise, home values and interest rates go up. After a while, you've forgotten all about that nice little section of land you own. Before you know it, your initial investment is much more than you dreamed."

"I don't know, John," Heather blinked her eyes, "I really don't understand all those investment values and interest rate things."

"You don't have to," John said, earnestly. "That's what you have me for."

"I do?"

"Why, of course. I can keep track of what's happening with your property. You don't have to worry about it at all."

Heather pursed her lips. "Would you need all of my ten thousand dollars? Can't I keep a teensy-weensy bit?"

"Well, you would make less of an investment that way. Of course, that would mean you would get much less a return. I suggest that you invest all of it to get the greatest return possible. I mean, this is money you weren't really expecting to have. Money you're getting for spending a week in a nice house. Anytime life hands you money like that, the best you can do is turn it into more money. That's what I want to do for you."

"Well, that's awfully sweet of you," Heather cooed.

"I just want you to be happy. And with this kind of

investment, you're sure to come out ahead."

Paul walked into the Kitchen again and noticed the familiar paperwork spread out over the table. "It's a pretty good deal, ain't it?"

"Yes, Mr. Polecat, it sounds like a real nice deal to me. I think it's just wonderful that John is sharing this with us."

"Please, ma'am," Paul began, taking a huge bite out of some food he found in the basement, "just call me Polecat. Ain't no 'mister' about it." He opened the refrigerator and chugged down half a container of orange juice.

Heather looked at him in disgust as he put the nearly empty carton back into the refrigerator. "I'll call you 'just Polecat' if you don't use the word 'ma'am' with me anymore."

He took another bite of food and spoke with his mouth full, "I'm just trying to mind muh good manners."

"Well, don't. 'Ma'am' makes me sound like I'm old."

"And you're certainly not old," John complimented.

"Why, thank you, John, that's very kind of you to say so." As she said this, Heather placed her fingertips ever so slightly upon his hand.

"Fine, if that's the way ya want it, miss Heather," Paul said, and walked out of the kitchen still gnawing away at whatever it was he was eating.

"That man is so disgusting," Heather said. "Why do you think he wants to be called Polecat, anyway?"

John smiled. "Probably just a nickname, my dear."

"Well, whatever could it mean?"

"If I remember correctly, I believe it is slang for describing a skunk."

Heather giggled again. "Well, it certainly is fitting," she said.

CHAPTER SEVEN

Gerald emerged from the foot of the stairs that led to the basement, out of breath. He shut the door behind him and leaned on it as if to keep something from escaping. "I was just going to get a candy bar," he gasped, as Jack and Gail came up from the living room. "I swear I didn't do it."

"What's the problem, Gerald?" Jack asked.

"I swear, Jack, it's not my fault! I just brushed against the thing and it flew apart."

"What isn't your fault?" Jack demanded, growing irritated with Gerald's desire to cover himself rather than divulge the problem.

With a hard grimace, Gerald slowly opened the door, keeping himself attached to it like a permanent fixture. Immediately, the sound of rushing water could be heard from within the basement. "Oh my God, the food!" Gail cried.

They rushed down the stairs with Gerald following slowly, keeping a distance. Jack hesitated at the foot of the stairs where water covered the entire floor. Off to the far wall, a large pipe with a big, red valve was gushing water six feet sideways into the air. The food was stored on one end of the basement, in an assortment of boxes and bags. Most of the items were in bulk and the rising water was already damaging large bags of flour and sugar.

Jack quickly splashed through the water and tried to turn the shut-off valve where the water seemed to be escaping from. It was stuck.

"I barely touched it," Gerald yelled from the stairs. Gail splashed over to the food and tried to drag a fifty-pound bag of sugar.

"Gerald," Jack yelled, "tell the others. Try to find the main shut-off. It should be outside somewhere. Wherever the pump is...and get as many towels as you can." He grasped the valve again and turned with all his might whereas it promptly broke off in his hand, shooting out even more water and nearly knocking him down.

"Jack, we've got to do something about this food," Gail called to him.

"Yeah, I know. This basement is so small, it will fill up in no time. Who in their right mind," he said, heaving a large bag of flour up from the water, "puts that size water pipe in a basement?"

***

Heather crossed her arms and rolled her eyes in irritation. "Slow down, Gerald. I have no idea what you're talking about."

"We've got to find the shut-off valve! The main water shut-off. The food's getting ruined. Oh, man, I didn't do this...I know I didn't do this."

Paul ran up and John came around the corner to see what all the commotion was about. "The basement's floodin'," Paul said, "we gotta find a way to shut off the water."

"My word," John gasped, "shouldn't there be some sort of main supply switch somewhere?"

Gerald was throwing his arms up in exasperation. "That's what I said. We have to turn it off somehow. Towels! Oh, man, I have to find some towels."

Paul turned to him with a seriousness that seemed almost frightening. "You round up some towels, Gerald," he said. "We'll find the valve."

As they all flew away from her, Heather winced. "The basement is flooding?"

***

Jack pushed at the pipe with the palm of his hand, trying to fight the water pressure. It was too strong. Gail was trying to salvage the smaller items now, wading through the water that was now lapping at her knees. Heather carefully descended the stairs with her high heels and almost shrieked when she saw the water. "My God, Jack, what on earth did you do?"

Gail half-turned and heaved some more containers at the dry edge of the stairs where a clutter of others rested. "He didn't do this," she yelled up at her. "I could use some help down here."

Heather looked down at the rising water and raised her eyebrows in surprise. "Oh, no. I'm not getting in that...that sewage."

"For crying out loud, Heather, it's fresh water," Jack yelled at her.

She straightened at the tone of his voice and lifted her chin. "Well, can't you do something, Jack? Can't you turn it off?"

Jack clenched his teeth hard. "No, Heather, I *can't* turn it off. Can't you see it's broken? Are you that much of a bimbo, you can't see what's going on here?"

"Bimbo! I'll show you 'bimbo' when you get out of there."

"Heather," Gail called in an exhaustive voice, "can you at least pick up that food and get it upstairs?" She pointed at the items closest to the rising water on the stairwell.

"Jack, you have some nerve," Heather said, as she descended a little further. "You do something like this and then you want to yell at me? Do you want to know something? You're a royal pain in the--" At that instant, she lost her footing and slipped on the wet steps. She yelled as her backside hit the stairway and she bumped down a couple of steps before falling straight into the water.

***

"Well I'll be," Paul said, running his fingers thoughtfully through his beard. They had traced the main pipeline all the way to a nearby stream. In the last rays of sunlight, they now stood in fascination at the sight before them. A large contraption of pipes and tanks were built into the embankment. Next to it was a large water wheel that seemed to be powering the pump. The water was then forced into some type of filtering unit and then released into a main supply pipe.

"Do you think we can stop this wheel?" John asked.

Paul looked at him for a second. "You wanna jump in there and stop it?"

John looked back at the wheel, forcing himself to realize the sheer power it was under. "I see your point. Well, we can't shut this pump off, either. This whole setup seems to be self-powered."

"Wait a minute," Paul said quickly. "I've got an idea." He followed the stream down a ways until he found what he was looking for. When he returned, he was dragging a large dead tree limb. "This just may do the trick," he grunted.

"Why, that's an excellent idea," John said.

"Don't be bragging 'bout my ingenuity just yet," Paul said. "Give me a hand, will ya?"

The two men edged toward the water wheel with the tree limb. On Paul's count of three, they hurled the limb between the spokes and watched as the wheel carried the limb upwards and crashed down on the top of the filtering unit. It wedged tightly and the wheel came to an abrupt halt.

"We did it!" John said, shaking Paul's hand.

"You bet we did," Paul agreed. "The only problem now is we won't have no water. If we can fix that busted pipe, then we'll come back and get this wheel going again."

***

Heather stood up, completely soaked with her arms out from her sides. Her face seemed to be displaying a number of contorted expressions and it looked like she was going to burst into tears at any second. "My...my dress is ruined."

"Oh, good grief," Jack said. "Get back upstairs and find Gerald."

"My dress..."

"Jack!" Gail pointed at the wall near the stairwell. There was a large gray box mounted there with conduit coming out of the top, climbing up the wall and disappearing through the ceiling; the water level was nearly up to an electrical circuit box.

"Alright," Jack said, "everybody out."

Gail waded quickly through the water until she found the steps. Heather stood there, grief-stricken until Jack grabbed her and pulled her towards the stairs.

"Get your hands off me!"

"Quit fighting me, Heather, we've got to get out of this water," Jack said, trying to keep hold of her squirming body.

"I swear, Jack if you don't let go of me I'll--" She thrust a knee between his legs.

Jack groaned in pain and fell backward into the water.

Gail turned from her ascent to see Jack disappearing below the surface. "Heather, what the hell did you do to him?" She went back in after him.

"He attacked me," Heather said, clambering up the wet steps. "I had to do something."

Jack came back up for air as Gail reached him. She helped guide him back to the steps as he groaned in agony. Her face wore a scowl as she looked up at Heather, who was kicking boxes of food back down into the water as she made her way hastily up the stairs. Gerald suddenly appeared at the top of the steps. "Hey, I found some towels."

He stopped short when he saw them. They were all soaked from head to toe. Heather was right in front of him, her hair an uncommon mess and black makeup running from her eyes. Gail and Jack were still climbing up the stairs on all fours. They all glared at him. He thrust his arms outward, offering the towels. "Uh, looks like you could really use these."

***

It was nearly dark as John and Paul continued to admire their handy work. "Free water," John was saying, "now there's a concept."

"It's the only way to go," Paul said, looking at the pumping unit. "The day I have to pay for water is the day they can haul me off in a buggy."

John looked at Paul curiously. "Haul you off in a--"

"So this thing don't use no electricity at all?"

"Yes, that's what I was saying," John replied. "It's completely self-sufficient. Come to think of it, I don't remember seeing power lines anywhere near the house."

They looked back towards the house. Sure enough, the area was clear of the usual heavy lines that might have drooped from a nearby power pole.

Paul rubbed his beard again. "Well, what the heck is powerin' the place?"

Just then, all the lights in the house flickered momentarily before they went completely out.

CHAPTER EIGHT

It was completely dark now. John groped around for the door to his room. He had made it up the stairs, which he thought was an accomplishment in itself. On his way, he literally bumped into Gerald, who filled him in on what happened in the basement. Once he found a door, he opened it cautiously and ran his hands along the wall for guidance. He could hear some movement in the room. "Gail, is that you?"

He heard a small laugh. "I'm afraid you've stumbled into the wrong room, Mr. Forest."

"Oh! Heather...forgive me, I must have lost my bearings. I can't see a thing in this pitch black."

She moved over to him and put a hand on his shoulder. "That's quite alright. I don't mind that you found my room."

John nervously took her hand from his shoulder. "Heather, I...my goodness, you are soaking wet."

"Yes, I should get out of these clothes, shouldn't I?"

"Uh, yes," John said, nervously, "you really should change. You could catch cold."

Heather laughed again. It was a small, seductive laugh.

"Heather, I..."

There was a sudden storm of footsteps from the outside hallway. "Get away from my husband, you little hussy!"

Gail said as she lunged for Heather. In her attack, she knocked her husband out of the way and the two women hit the floor with a thud. A series of grunts and high-pitched shrieks could be heard as the two tumbled across the wooden floor. John hunched over and tried to find the two women, but they were moving too fast. Just when he thought he was getting close, a flying fist hit him square in the nose, knocking him backward into the dresser. He hit something hard with his knee and yelled in pain. Holding his leg and hopping on one foot in the dark, he let out with a string of exasperated profanities.

The women were on their feet again. One of them managed to push the other out of the room onto the handrail that overlooked the living room. The fight continued there and soon they were rolling around again. John hopped out into the hall, straining to try to see them. He knew he had to stop them somehow, so he got down on his hands and knees and painfully crawled over to the heart of the ferocity. He nearly got kicked in the head with a swinging leg, but caught it smartly and started to pull with all his might.

Loud footsteps were hurrying up the stairs now. "What the hell is going on?"

"Jack, we've got to stop them. They're going to kill each other."

"Alright, now! Break it up," Jack commanded. He reached down into the furious mass and grabbed hold of one of the frantically twisting bodies. As he tried to pry one body away from the other, he realized one of his hands was cupped around something round and firm under a wet shirt.

"Let go of me, you pervert!" Heather wailed and kicked at him. He felt a hard blow to his ankle and let go of his grasp. Instinctively, he put most of his weight on his other foot. Heather let out with another unsuspecting kick and caught him hard in his other leg. Jack stepped back, wincing with pain. His foot caught the first step of the stairs and he felt himself falling backward as if in slow motion. Then he felt a hard crack as his head came down with a thud on the stairs and he began to go into a roll. A rumble not unlike thunder proceeded, coupled with deep gasps and grunts as Jack rolled down the long staircase in pitch black. He managed to catch part of the handrail at the very last, which only succeeded in making the rest of his journey a bumpy back ride. He came to rest on the bottom floor, his head hanging over the step to the living room.

The house was suddenly silent.

Then, John's hoarse voice broke out from above. "Jack! Jack, are you alright?"

Gerald and Paul, having heard all the commotion, came in just in time to hear Jack's fall. Paul knelt down and felt for Jack's arm. "Jack, say something. C'mon, buddy."

Gerald stood there, trying to see in the darkness. "Is he...?"

"He's alive," Paul said quickly, "but I think he's knocked out or something." A bit louder, he said, "Anybody got any medical training?"

"Don't move him," Gail called down to him. "His back could be broken."

"I'm not gonna move him," Paul said, irritated, "but we need to do something."

"Gerald," John said, "why don't you go see if you can find some candles."

"I am...I mean, that's what I was trying to do anyway." He left for the kitchen.

Heather stood up and put her fingernails between her teeth. "He...he's going to be alright. Right? I didn't think I kicked him that hard. I mean..."

Paul looked up to where her voice was coming from. "You done this to him?"

"I didn't mean to kick him down the stairs. I mean, how was I supposed to know he would lose his balance?"

Gail glared at her in the darkness. She almost said something but didn't want to rekindle their fight. At least not right now.

"Wait a minute, he's trying to say something," Paul said and bent down to hear.

"Heather," came the whisper.

"Miss Heather, I think you better get down here," Paul said, standing up.

She moved nervously to the top of the stairs. "What...what is it?"

Paul's eyes bulged in the darkness. "I don't know, woman. He's asking for you, trying to say something. Why don't you get down here and find out what it is?"

She made her way carefully down the stairs, unsure of wanting to go near him. Finally, she moved to his side. "I'm here, Jack."

"Heather," the whisper came again, barely audible.

She moved her ear close to his mouth. "I'm here, Jack. Talk to me."

In a low, but clearly audible voice he said, "If you kick me one more time, I swear it will be the last thing you do."

Heather quickly stood up and let out a throaty sound of disgust. "I should have known it! Nothing can hurt his thick skull."

The others breathed a sigh of relief. Gerald walked in with some candles and lit them in the living room. The entire place took on an eerie glow as shadows flickered on the walls. Paul helped Jack up. Bruised, but not badly hurt, he limped into the living room and let himself fall onto the sofa. Heather sat down in the recliner. Her hair was still a mess and her clothes were still a little wet, but she was too tired to do anything about it. Gail came down the stairs, followed distantly by her husband and they took a seat on the sofa with Jack. Gail wore a scowl, aimed perpetually at Heather. Paul took his place by the fireplace mantel and Gerald, lighting his last candle, sat in the other recliner near Heather.

"Where do you think ol' combat woman is?" Paul asked.

Heather rolled her eyes. "Probably out hunting cat."

"At least she's not out hunting someone else's husband," Gail said sharply.

"I'm not after your husband! Believe me, sweetheart, if I was I would have already had him."

John pushed both hands together into a quick point. "Please...please, will you stop arguing? This entire thing is ridiculous."

"You can say that again," Paul said. "You city people don't have much sense when it comes to dealing with a crisis."

"Just what exactly are you trying to say, Paul?" Gail wanted to know.

"You know what I'm saying. You people ain't got a lick of sense when it comes down to the basics of life. You're all so wrapped up in your own world, you don't have a clue how to see things as they are."

"So, tell us, Paul," Jack said evenly, "what exactly are we missing?"

Paul let out a sigh to dismiss the question. "I ain't got much of an education, but I had to learn a lot about life the hard way. You people are smart when it comes to numbers and social graces, but I bet none of you could survive one day out there in them woods."

"And this is a bad thing?" Heather said.

"There's so much crap that goes on in the city," Paul continued, "that you forget how to be a human being. It'll corrupt you. I know that because I've been there."

"I haven't spent my whole life in the city," Jack said, "but I've lived there long enough to know it's just like anywhere else. There's good and bad in everyone. You're making generalizations that don't amount to anything."

"Maybe there is some truth to what he's saying," Gail said slowly.

"What?" Jack asked, surprised.

Gail looked at her husband and sighed to herself. "Why don't you tell them?"

"What do you mean? Tell them what?" John said, irritated.

"You know exactly what I'm talking about," Gail said, her eyes shining with a kind of resolution.

"Gail, this is not the time or the place-"

"Tell them," she demanded. "Or I will."

John was silent for a moment. Then he sighed, stood up and shoved his hands in his pockets. He slowly paced the floor while all eyes in the room followed his movements in the flickering half-light. Finally, he stopped and looked down at the floor. "We're not as 'well to do' as we lead people to believe," he said.

"We're broke," Gail said, soberly.

Heather's eyebrows raised and her mouth opened a little. Gerald looked at them curiously. "Well, there's nothing wrong with being broke," he said. "I've been broke all my life, but I always manage to make it somehow."

"That's not all of it," Gail said.

"Gail, please. We don't have to talk about this here."

Gail wrenched her hands together. When she spoke, there was a kind of anger in her voice accompanied by a quiver. "I am really tired of living like this. I'm tired of living a lie and lying to people."

"Gail, please..." John began.

"We don't have any money," she continued in a shaky voice. "Not anymore because my husband gambled it all away. No, not at the casino, not at the races. He gambled it away with high-risk investment schemes. It's funny, you know..." Her voice trailed off. She walked over to one of the candles and watched the flickering light, not wanting to face the others.

John stared down at the floor. "The first one's paid off," he said, "they paid off big. It seemed like I couldn't lose. But when I kept on trying, I did lose. It only made me want to try harder, to recapture that excitement. So, I kept on trying and I kept losing. Soon, I was taking out loans to get investment money, certain that the next one would pay off."

"It never did," Gail continued, "and soon we were buried in debt..."

"What about filing for bankruptcy?" Jack offered.

John took a deep breath. "I still believed we could make our way out of it. I didn't want to ruin our credit for years to come. I was still investing and there was no way I could do that with bad credit."

"We kept borrowing and borrowing," Gail added. "Soon, we were borrowing from friends because our 'funds were tied up'. When we ran out of friends, we turned to strangers..." She looked down at the candle again. "...and promised them a high return for their investment."

Jack nodded slowly. "For an investment in real estate."

"Yes," Gail said, her eyes glassy, "real estate that doesn't even exist."

Heather looked at John with a hurt expression. "You were going to con me into buying land that doesn't exist?"

"This whole thing was a perfect opportunity," John said dryly. "We get paid to come here and, in the process, we could get investment money out of each and every one of you."

"No offense, John, but I never did buy into your scheme," Jack said. "I've always believed that if something sounds too good to be true, it usually is."

"There have been a lot of people who didn't fall for it," John admitted. "But there's been a lot that have. What have I become? This is not the kind of person I am. I've always made honest business deals and earned a lot of money in the process. In losing everything, I suppose I panicked. I was willing to do anything to get back to where we were in the beginning, bringing my wife down with me and obliterating the trust of others."

John looked up at the others, his demeanor quite opposite from his steadfast posture and quick, intelligent thinking. "Heather, Polecat...I am truly sorry. I've betrayed your trust and insulted your intelligence by attempting to swindle you out of your money."

Paul rubbed his finger under his nose and waved his hand out in a gesture of indifference. "No harm done. You didn't really con me, 'cause I never gave you no money. Besides, sounds like you learnt your lesson."

John sat back down on the couch and Gail, her face a mixture of sadness and relief, sat beside him. "I *have* learned my lesson," he said. "We're just going to have to find a way to get out of this hole I've put us in."

Gail put her hand on his. "We'll find a way."

Paul picked up his rifle from the corner near the fireplace and headed towards the door.

"Where are you going, Polecat?" Heather asked.

"Going huntin', miss Heather. We're gonna need something to eat. Besides, I can't hang around here all night and listen to you people spill yer guts."

"You're going hunting at this time of night?" Jack asked.

"Yep. I'll find me a nice, cozy spot in the woods and sleep until it just starts getting light. If I fall asleep here, I'll wake up too late and won't get anything."

CHAPTER NINE

After Paul was gone, Jack decided to break the sudden silence. "So, what's your story, 'miss' Heather."

"What do you mean, 'what's my story'?"

"I'm sure you have a few skeletons in your closet."

"I don't have a story, Jack, but I'm sure you have a few to tell."

"It seems everyone has some fault or problem," John said, feeling relieved that the attention was turned from him. "Perhaps we could talk about it and help each other."

"I don't need help," Heather retorted. "But if you want to help someone, why don't you go find that army woman. My shrink could make a fortune off of her."

"Your shrink?" Jack asked, as if finding a secret doorway.

"Yes, I see a psychiatrist, big deal. Who doesn't these days? It's sort of a requirement for steady health, like seeing a dentist."

Jack leaned forward on the couch. "I don't go to one. Anyone else?"

The others shook their heads.

"Well, you ought to," she said to Jack. "Anyone can see you have problems."

"I'm interested in your problems," Jack pressed. "Why do you need to see a shrink?"

"I told you, it's no big deal," Heather said defensively.

"I know they cost a lot," Gerald said. "Why spend all that money if you don't really need to?"

"Sometimes..." Heather stood up. "Sometimes, I just need to get things off my chest, you know?"

"What kind of things?" Jack prodded.

"When people get too much to take, it helps to talk about it to someone."

"So why not just talk to a friend?" Gail asked with disinterested irritation.

"Because you have to talk about it with someone who understands what you're going through. You know what? I don't know why I'm even talking about this. It's none of your business anyway."

"You're right," John said, "it's not our business. But it doesn't really matter because we're all more or less strangers to each other. Sometimes it helps to talk to a complete stranger."

"I haven't gone back to her in a while," she said with a nervous laugh. "She started digging for things, you know? Making up problems that I didn't have just to solve them."

"Sounds like a quack," Gerald said.

"Yeah," Heather laughed in agreement. "She told me I had the tendency to lean on people, to use them to suit my own needs. Ridiculous!"

"That sounds pretty harsh," Jack said, leaning back in the couch, "even for a psychiatrist. On what facts did she base those findings?"

Heather put her hands on the back of the recliner she had been sitting in. "I don't know, I think she just made them up. She would drag out her notes and recite some convoluted experience I told her about. It was usually about the way I treated my friends. She said that instead of a give and take friendship, I start off with 'how can you be to my benefit?' and when they didn't suit my needs, I shut them out.

"Isn't that stupid? I mean, I have always been there for my friends. *I'm* the one that gets shut out. *I'm* the one that gets ignored. They're the ones who should be going to see a shrink. Maybe then, they could see they're not as perfect as they think they are."

"You may not think you have a problem, Heather," Gail said, "but I think you do."

"Thanks a lot, miss perfect."

"I know I'm not perfect, but you won't admit you're not. Just what exactly did you want from my husband?"

Heather rolled her eyes. "Oh, please. Are you going to start this again?"

"Yes, I am. I want to know what you hoped to accomplish. If you had any sense at all, you knew I wasn't very far away. Did you think you could steal him away from me with some spur-of-the-moment fling, or what?"

"Maybe I wanted to get caught," Heather cried angrily. "Maybe if somebody caught me and beat some sense into me, I would stop."

"Stop doing what?" Gail demanded.

"Stop manipulating people," Heather shouted, moving towards the couple. "When I saw your husband, I saw money. I haven't lived in the lap of luxury all my life like some people, but I've been there. And I like it. I saw you and your husband drive up here in that nice car. The clothes you wear, the things you say. I don't understand why I have to live the way I do and some people get it handed to them on a silver platter!"

"Silver platter," John said, amused. "If only it were that easy."

Gail laughed genuinely. "You were after his money? Now, that's funny. We're flat broke and you were gold-digging."

"Well, how was I supposed to know that?"

Jack rubbed his forehead as if trying to ward off an impending headache. "Now I'm confused. You say that you don't understand why you have to live the way you do. Yet, you have that nice little sports car out there and enough money to pay a psychiatrist. Sounds like you're doing pretty well to me."

"Well, just maybe I want to raise my standards higher

than what I'm accustomed to. And as for my car, that's another thing. There's no telling what damage has been done because of your truck."

Jack shook his head and rolled his eyes.

Gail looked at Jack. "What is she talking about?"

"She ran into the back of my pickup truck," Jack explained, "and she thinks it's my fault."

"It is your fault," Heather asserted and turned towards the others, "If he'd pulled his truck all the way into the drive, I never would've hit it."

John straightened up. "You mean where it's parked now?"

"Yes, it's in the same place," Heather said, "go look."

"I know where it's at," John said. "I must say, Jack, she does have a point. Your tail end is sticking pretty far out. I might have hit it myself with an extra blink of the eye."

"Yeah," Gerald agreed, "with the dust coming off of that dirt road, I only saw it at the last minute. But I wasn't going that fast anyway."

"Are you people serious?" Jack asked, incredulously. "My truck was parked. She hit it. It was her fault."

Gail said, "Well, it was just an accident. It's nobody's fault, really."

"I'll tell you what," Heather said, turning to Jack with her arms crossed, "if you pay half, I'll pay half."

"I'm not going to pay for something I didn't do!"

"It sounds like a reasonable solution," John said.

"Yeah, she's willing to meet you halfway," Gerald said.

Jack threw his hands in the air. "Fine! I'll pay half. Are you satisfied?"

Heather turned and went back to her chair with a self-satisfied smile on her face.

In the space of silence that followed, John clasped his hands together and said, "Well, Gerald, my boy, we all seem to be airing our dirty laundry here. What's your story?"

Gerald looked around at them nervously. He reddened slightly as if there was a giant spotlight on him. He could feel the warmth run like fire up his face and suddenly wished he were anywhere but in this room with everyone staring at him. "You...you guys don't want to hear about my problems," he said, squirming around in his seat.

"Sure we do," John said with enthusiasm and spread his arms out. "What else is there to do?"

"Well..." Gerald began. He was glad there was only the light from the candles to expose him. He already felt naked and embarrassed and he didn't think he could survive under normal lighting conditions. "...I guess if Heather's problem is using people, then I'm just the opposite. I let people use me. Actually, they walk all over me. I...I never really admitted it to myself until recently. I'm learning to be more honest to myself, I guess." Gerald paused and gave a quick glance at the others, wondering if there was any ridicule in their eyes. "When I talk to someone...anyone, they don't listen to me. Maybe they don't think I could have anything important to say..."

"That's ridiculous, Gerald," Gail said, "I'm sure people do listen to you."

"No," Gerald shook his head. "No, I know it for a fact. They hear my words, but they don't listen. And when I'm talking to someone and somebody else comes along, they just start talking, butting into the conversation like I wasn't even there."

Gerald stood up and pulled his arms in tightly until it seemed as if he were trying to hug himself. He moved behind the chair Heather was sitting in, further into the darkness. "I realize I'm a social outcast. For whatever reason, I don't flow in the same direction as most people. It's something I've learned to live with..."

Heather spoke up. "Gerald, if we were all the same, this world would be a very boring place."

Gerald let out a small, nervous laugh. "And a lonely one. I'm invisible to the naked eye. People look right through me and my words...when I speak it's like people have already decided to ignore whatever's coming out of my mouth, like I could never possibly have something important to say... " Gerald's voice cracked and it sounded like he ran out of breath.

The others looked at each other with worried expressions. Finally Gail said, "Gerald, it's okay, you don't have to talk about this if you don't want to."

Suddenly, Gerald spoke again. His voice was tainted with the hint of an emotional outpour; a dam that could break at any minute. "A couple of years ago, I almost did it. I almost put an end to it. I walked right in and got on the elevator and went to the highest floor I could get to. I wanted to go to the roof, but the door was locked. So, I found myself on the twenty-third floor. I walked around like some zombie through these business offices. I guess I got a few strange looks, but no one tried to stop me. All I wanted was a window, a damn ledge to step out on, but all the windows were reserved for offices with a view. And if I had been thinking straight, I would have realized that the building I was in didn't even have ledges. I couldn't even get that right."

Jack said, "Good Lord, Gerald, nothing's worth that."

"No?" Anger was added to the range of emotions that engulfed Gerald's words. "You try living everyday just to please everybody else. Making sure you don't offend anyone. Being sure they don't take what you say the wrong way. Knowing when to talk, when not to, when you're saying too much and when you haven't said enough. I have this...'buffer' up here." He jabbed some fingers into his forehead. "I can't just say what I'm thinking. I have to think about what I'm thinking and make sure it'll be accepted. I have to check it first to make sure it's funny and interesting enough. By the time I figure out what I should say, it's no longer relevant. So I either say nothing and look like an idiot or say what finally comes to mind and look like an even bigger idiot."

He turned towards the fireplace now, his face hidden from view. When he spoke again, his voice carried the sound of pain. "I feel like I have so much inside of me. So much to tell, so much to give. I think all the time. I think so much that I wonder if I'm going crazy. But every time I try to open up to someone, I get shot down. I get criticized and patronized and ridiculed for whatever I'm thinking. And I..." Gerald turned to face the others. His eyes were glassy and he began shaking an angry fist near his chest. "...I take it all in. I back down and let them patronize me. I let them sympathize and I let them pat me on the shoulder. And I want to please everyone so bad, I smile and let them think they made it better, but it never gets better..."

Gerald stopped and turned away again.

Jack had a cigarette in his fingers. He thought about lighting it up then tucked it in his shirt pocket. "Gerald, we all have things that drive us to the edge sometimes. This life isn't easy, that's for sure. It pushes you hard sometimes, but you have to learn to push back. Whatever doesn't kill us makes us stronger..."

Heather was looking at Jack in an expression of disbelief. "Jack, you're doing exactly what he's been talking about. You're patronizing him, telling him everything will be alright."

He leaned forward, squinting at her. "What I was trying to do is tell him that we all have problems. We all have to face this crap at one time or another."

"How can you say that? You don't have the slightest idea what he's going through. None of us do."

"I think maybe she's right, Jack," Gail said. "There's no way we could know what he's going through."

John pursed his lips. "Well, I don't know. I've come pretty close to the edge. I've thought about doing myself in at times..."

Gail raised her eyebrows and looked at her husband.

Gerald suddenly appeared from out of the darkness. He spread his arms open. "You see? See what I'm talking about? I'm right here. You're talking about me like I was in Kansas! I'm right *here*."

"Yes, of course you are," Gail empathized, "we know that. It's just that we want to help you, but we don't know how."

Gerald shook his head. "You don't have to help me. I

don't need your help. I guess...I guess I just needed to get this out of my system. I didn't mean to blurt all that stuff out. I don't know where it came from. It just came out. Just feeling a little sorry for myself, I guess."

Heather looked up at him. "Now you're doing it."

He looked at her, puzzled. "What?"

"You're doing exactly what you said. You're backing down. You're belittling what you said just so we'll feel better about it."

"No. Honestly, Heather, I'm not," Gerald said.

"Yes you are."

"No, I'm not."

Gail asked, "Are you sure, Gerald?"

Gerald scratched his head and seemed to be taking an inventory of his personal feelings. "Yeah, I'm pretty sure. Actually, I feel a lot better. I'm sorry for going off the handle like that. I guess I just needed to get it out of my system."

Jack retrieved his cigarette again and lit it this time. "No need to apologize, Gerald. It helps to talk about things."

Heather rolled her eyes and then scrutinized Jack. "Okay, Jack. It's your turn."

Jack let out a casual puff of smoke. "No. It's not."

"Now, Jack," Gail said, "we've all let our defenses down and told our stories."

"There's no story to tell."

"Sure there is," John said. "You said yourself, we all come close to the edge sometimes."

"Yes, we do. I guess I've been lucky because I haven't been through anything that can compare with..."

"Shhhh!" Gail hissed suddenly and then whispered, "Did you hear that?"

"I didn't hear anything," Gerald whispered back.

"It sounded like it came from upstairs," Gail said.

Heather looked up towards the top of the stairs. "I swear, if that woman's crawling around in the attic again..."

John stood up, stretched and yawned. "Well, she better not make any more noise because I've got to get some rest."

He looked at his watch. "My word. It's nearly two in the morning. Where did the time go?"

"It's been a long night," Jack agreed and eyed Heather. "After nearly drowning and getting electrocuted in the basement and getting kicked down a flight of stairs, I'm ready for some sleep."

While the others were heading off to bed, Gerald decided to get some fresh air before he turned in. He walked out onto the back deck and braced his arms on the wooden railing. He stared out at the darkness and listened to the night sounds from the woods.

Man, I can't believe I went off like that, he thought. *What in the world got into me?*

He pushed a hand up his forehead and over his hair, feeling the cool night air refresh him. He started to turn and go back inside, but then he heard a noise. It was distant at first, but seemed to be coming closer. At first, he thought he was imagining it, but no, there it was again. A 'meowing' sound was coming from out of the woods.

"Kitty!" Gerald moved quickly down the steps and squinted into the darkness. He could only see what little the moonlight illuminated, but soon he was able to make out the small form of a cat. It seemed to be in a hurry, anxious to get back home from whatever journey it had taken in the forest. It almost ran right up the steps, but stopped when it spied Gerald standing there.

Gerald squatted down and offered out an inviting hand. "Here, kitty, kitty," he soothed. The cat looked up at him, alert. Then it looked around, scoping out possible avenues of escape. Gerald coaxed the cat again. "It's alright, kitty...come on." Ever so carefully, the cat moved towards him, its blue eyes shining with curiosity. Gerald wanted to reach out and grab it, but opted to restrain from making any sudden movements, wanting to gain the cat's trust. Then, after soft fur brushed against his leg, he slowly reached down and picked up the feline. "There...that wasn't so bad, was it?" He cradled the cat in his arms and stood up.

Making his way back onto the deck, he heard another noise and looked up. It sounded like something was on the side of the house. Then there was a strong 'thud' on the ground. A form came from out of the darkness, moving swiftly and with purpose. It took Gerald a moment to recognize the camouflaged figure. Sensing the danger to his newfound friend, he headed for the back door. She was quick. Grabbing him by the shoulder, she pulled him over to the corner of the deck and pushed him up against the wall.

"Where do you think you're going in such a hurry?"

Gerald held the cat closely to him in an ill attempt at hiding the furry creature. "I'm just going into the house. What were you doing up there?"

"That's none of your business," she said, poking a finger at the furry substance squirming between Gerald's arms. "What do we have here?"

"Leave it alone," Gerald said. "She hasn't done anything to you."

"Hasn't done anything? You see this cut on my face? I'll probably be scarred for life because of this little bitch. Now hand her over."

"No. You'll hurt her," Gerald protested.

"I'll hurt you if you don't hand it over!"

Gerald's voice quivered when he spoke, but he was determined to protect the animal. "You're...you're not getting her."

The army woman held his shoulder easily against the corner wall with one hand. She withdrew an object from her belt and brought it up to Gerald's face. The knife glimmered in the moonlight. She twirled it slowly between her fingers. "Do you really think she's worth it? Give me the feline and I'll let you go."

"What...what are you going to do, cut me?" Gerald could feel beads of sweat forming on his forehead.

"I don't have to do anything as long as you hand over the rodent."

A calm resolution came into Gerald's demeanor and it was reflected in his voice. "No. I won't let you hurt her."

"Gerald," she said with a sigh and smiled deviously, moving her face very close to his, "you're so brave putting your life on the line for this useless ball of fur." She moved the edge of the blade lightly over the stubble on his face and looked at him quizzically. "You ever been with a woman, Gerald?"

"Why do you care?" He said, his voice starting to quiver again.

"I don't care. I was just wondering...because it would be a shame," she said, slicing off one of his chin hairs, "that such a handsome young man would have to die a useless death before experiencing the pleasures that life has to offer."

Gerald straightened himself, feeling a surge of the same anger he experienced earlier. "You can threaten me with the knife. You probably fight better than I ever could, so you could beat me up if you want to. But you're going to have to kill me if you want this cat."

Her eyes studied his for a moment, squinting with a kind of vengeful anger. She grabbed the back of his head and pushed his lips onto hers. She kissed him deeply and forcefully then withdrew with an insane little laugh. "You're lucky," she said, pushing back from him, "that I don't have time for this."

She left as quickly as she had come and Gerald noticed as she ran off into the night that she was wearing a small backpack. He stood there against the wall, still clutching the cat tightly to him until he noticed it was squirming for air. He lessened his hold and breathed out a long sigh of relief.

CHAPTER TEN

The large oriental vase fell through the air as if in slow motion. For an instant, its beauty was still intact. The intricate designs and gold linings were still a monument to an artist's handiwork. The perfectly smooth surface still reflected hints of the first sunlight of the morning.

In another instant, time suddenly speeding up, the priceless object came crashing to the cold hard floor. It shattered, spreading out evenly from the center of destruction. Finally, the broken pieces came to rest, littering the floor like so much garbage.

Every pair of sleeping eyes in the house snapped open.

"What in tarnation did you do that for?" Paul's voice bellowed with anger and irritation.

Jack appeared at the top of the stairs, squinting and still tying his robe. Then, Gerald came out like a zombie and stood beside Jack as if he'd been called out for morning reveille. Soon, John and Gail emerged from their room and Heather could be heard grumbling down the hall before she stood with the rest of them, arms crossed and wondering what they were all looking at.

Down in the living room, the army woman was standing near the fireplace with a thousand broken pieces of ceramic at her feet. Her chest was rising and falling with short, hostile breaths. Paul stood inside the front door with his gun leveled on her.

"My word," John said.

Irritation consumed Jack's gruff voice. "Alright, what the hell is going on here?"

"I just got back from huntin'. I caught our little friend here under yer truck."

"What?" Jack rubbed his eyes, trying to wake up. "Was she looking for bugs there, too?"

"No," Paul said, "she weren't looking fer no bugs. She cut yer fuel line. And everybody else's near as I can tell."

Jack was moving down the stairs now with the others parading behind him. He stared at the army woman as he moved, his eyes narrowing. "You cut the fuel line on my truck? Why?"

She didn't answer him but continued looking at Paul with extreme prejudice. Everyone was in the living room now and Gail pushed her way to the front. "Polecat, is it really necessary to hold that gun on her? Why don't you put it down and we can all talk."

"Keep it on her, Polecat," Jack said. "Sorry, Gail, but something is going on here and I don't think she will listen to reason."

"You got that right," Paul said, grimacing. "I got her in here and the first thing she did was go and smash that vase. She's a wild one alright."

Jack faced her, arms crossed and stern like a father to a daughter who's been out too late. "So, what's the story? Why did you sabotage our vehicles?"

She didn't move or make an attempt to answer. She only stood there, burning in anger and glaring at Paul.

"I'll tell ya what I think," Paul said, his eyes filled with suspicion, "I think she was planning on leaving our little party and didn't want anybody coming after her."

"That's absurd," Heather said, "why would we even want to go after her?"

"Yeah," Paul agreed, "why would we indeed. How 'bout we see what you got in that little knapsack of yers?"

When she still made no effort to respond, Paul walked

purposely to her. There was a kind of insanity in his eyes. He could move quickly when he wanted to. The combination of his expression and his quick movement with the gun was somewhat alarming for all of them. All except the army woman, who looked as if she could chew nails.

Paul turned her around and pressed the end of the barrel to her rear. Then, he quickly untied the fastener on her backpack. He reached in and pulled out his fist. He examined the contents close to his eyes for a second and then held them out for the others to see.

"Look familiar?" He asked them, not taking his eyes off the army woman.

"She took our valuables!" Gail said, astonished.

Gerald suddenly awakened. "It makes sense now. She must have been in the attic last night and I saw her come out with her backpack on."

Jack nodded his head. "And the flooding of the basement. A perfect diversion."

"I can't take credit for that," the army woman spat out, "but I was glad to take advantage of it."

"You're a common thief," John said.

"And you're a common idiot," she retorted. "You're a liar and a con man. Does that make you any better?"

John started to say something, then closed his mouth.

"Okay," Jack said, "let's have our belongings back." He stepped forward, intending to remove the pack, but Paul suddenly moved closer to the army woman. He put an arm around her neck and moved the barrel of his gun near her head.

"Don't nobody move," Paul said. The wild insanity look glazed over his eyes as he glanced nervously around at the others.

Jack stopped. "Polecat, what're you doing?"

"What's it look like I'm doing? I'm taking what I can get is what I'm doing."

"You don't have to do this, Polecat," Heather said, "this isn't the kind of person you are."

"Sorry, Miss Heather, but I need the money more than all

of you. Besides, you have no idea what kind of person I am."

"Paul, listen to reason," Gail insisted. "If you leave now, you won't get your ten thousand dollars. That's a lot more than whatever you'll get by stealing our belongings."

"Ain't gonna be no ten grand fer me anyhow. You see, I wasn't invited to this little shindig. Jack, gimme the keys to yer truck."

Jack stood glaring at Paul. "The keys are in the truck," he said.

Paul eyed them all, "Sorry to do this to you folks, but like I said, I'm kind of desperate for money at the moment. If I see any of you following me, the recruit here gets it."

Heather started for him. "Do you think I care if you shoot..."

Jack thrust out his arm in front of her. "Stop, Heather, he may just do it."

"You bet I will. Now, I'm just gonna ease on out of here."

He backed slowly towards the door with her, his large arm tight around her unseen neck. Her face was red from his grip, but there was no fear in her eyes. Just a blind fury.

"You'll never get away with this," Jack said.

"Paul stopped momentarily at the door. "C'mon, Jack, you can do better than that. That saying's older than the hills. Oh, by the way...if yall get hungry, there's a six-point out on the back deck. Bye, now."

***

They stood outside the door and watched as Paul drove off with his hostage. The two didn't get very far. A short ways down the dirt road, the truck engine spat, sputtered and coughed out the last drop of gas. Paul hopped out and kicked the side of the truck several times, cursing. When he finally settled down, he looked at the long dirt road. He appeared to be considering the thirty miles distance to town. Then, he laid his gun across the hood of the truck and put his head down on it.

Jack allowed a slight smile to curve his lips. There was no way Paul was going to make a clean get-away. He watched the hunched over figure at the truck. It seemed that Paul was never going to lift his head back up.

Perhaps he's thinking it over, thought Jack.

Down at the truck, Paul's eyes were closed tightly. He could feel the cold steel of the gun's metal pressing into his forehead. He was trying to think, to formulate a new plan of action. His mind was drawing a blank and he became more and more frustrated. Finally, he looked up and rested his arms and chin on the gun. He made himself relax. He had to try to think clearly. Staring blankly into the woods on the side of the road, a glint of something caught his eye. Something was reflecting the morning sunlight that, up to now, was doing little more than streaking the clouds with a pinkish hue.

Paul still didn't move. He squinted at the sharp reflection with dumbfounded curiosity. Inside the truck, the army woman looked at the expression on his face, seeing that he was staring intently at something. She shifted uncomfortably.

Suddenly, Paul snatched his gun from the hood and moved quickly over to where the shiny object was. "Oh, Mama!" He proclaimed.

There, hidden just under the brush, was the most beautiful motorcycle he had ever seen. He quickly pulled the brush away to reveal it in its entirety. The chrome sparkled from the handlebars to the mufflers. The elongated gas tank sported a deep blue with an airbrushed picture of wild horses charging outward like devil steeds on their way to freedom. The engine looked as if it were capable of nothing less than sheer power. The sleek, black seat had passenger room and saddlebags attached to the rear. Paul spotted the Harley-Davidson logo and thrust his arms skyward. "Thank you, Jesus, it's a Hawg!"

The truck door slammed behind him. "Don't you dare lay a hand on my bike."

With one strong arm, Paul stretched out the rifle straight at her. "What?" A look of deep suspicion crept into his expression. "Oh, now I get it. I was kinda wonderin' how you was gonna get away with yer loot. But now I see. Get all the goods, cut the gas lines and run down here to yer hidden motorcycle. Not a bad plan. Too bad I spoiled things fer ya. Who'd you steal this thing from, anyway?" He gave her a toothy grin, grabbed the handlebars and pulled the bike upright.

From up at the house, Heather strained to see what was happening down the dirt road. "What on earth are they doing?"

"I don't know," Jack said. "Looks like Polecat found something in the woods."

Paul wheeled the motorcycle out onto the sandy road. He took a second to look over its dazzling appearance out in the open. He slowly mounted it like a kid wanting to savor every moment of a brand new toy. The seat felt good as he rested his ample weight upon it. His arms stretched out to the handlebars instinctively and he felt a boyish excitement come over him. The bike felt like it was becoming part of him and he smiled lustfully.

He heard the army woman take a step and snapped back to reality, lifting the gun from his lap. He gestured with it, motioning her to come and join him.

She walked over and stopped in front of the bike. "I'll give you one chance," she said. "Get off the bike, give me the sack and let me ride out of here. If you don't, you'll soon regret it."

Paul gave out a loud chuckle and rested his gun barrel in the middle of the handlebars. He looked straight at her and shuddered with exaggeration. "I'm sooo scared," he said with mock seriousness. "Now get on the bike."

She complied and Paul pushed his shotgun through an opening in the handlebars. After positioning it several times, he found a place it could rest without slipping out. His finger found the start button and the bike roared to life. He could feel the immense power underneath him. The 'blub,

blub, blub' of the engine vibrated through his body, taking over his senses. The bike was truly a part of him now. He looked ahead and saw the untamed virgin road inviting him. He turned the throttle quickly a few times, getting the feel of the bike. The engine responded, sending a series of loud 'pops' into the air. He tapped the gearshift with his toe and slowly let out the clutch, simultaneously turning the throttle. Once the bike was in motion, he quickly accelerated. The wind pushed back his beard and long hair and a wide smile invaded his expression.

Back at the house, the others could only watch as the motorcycle and their belongings disappeared quickly down the dirt road in a cloud of dust.

CHAPTER ELEVEN

The stranded house residents sat gloomily around the living room. All except for Heather. She paced back and forth as the others looked on.

"How could this happen to me?" She asked rhetorically. "I mean, I try to do the right things. I can usually tell when somebody's up to something."

"In case you haven't noticed," Gail said strongly, "you're not the only one whose been had."

Heather continued, oblivious to Gail's statement. "What am I going to do now? No power. No way to get back to civilization. All the food's wet. What am I going to eat? What if I starve?"

"Polecat said something about some food on the back porch," Gerald offered.

"That's right!" Heather said, "And I'm hungry, too. What was it he said? Something about six-points or something like that? What does that mean?"

Jack sighed and the rest of them remained silent.

"Well," Heather insisted, "does anyone know what he was talking about?"

"Why don't you go out there and find out," Jack suggested bitterly.

"Fine. I think I'll just do that."

She took off towards the rear of the house. Jack held up

five fingers and counted them down, moving his lips silently. *Five, four, three, two...one.*

Heather screamed, sending up a shrill note that ended in something only dogs could hear. A rather large deer was sprawled over the railing of the deck. The side of its head was drenched in blood. The beautiful antlers were perfectly symmetrical, branching out to three points on either side. Heather turned and ran back into the house, taking quick, short steps with her hands held up to her cheeks. She stopped before the living room and tried to tell the others of the horrifying sight. She pointed towards the back of the house and mouthed the words, but no sounds came out. Finally, she said, "A-animal. There's a d-dead animal out there."

"Yeah," Jack said, "Polecat was such a nice guy, he brought us some food before he ripped us off. Anybody like deer meat?"

"It-it was a deer?" Heather cried, "Polecat killed Bambi?"

Jack, ignoring Heather's distress, turned to the others and said, "Polecat caught her in the middle of cutting our fuel lines. Maybe she didn't finish the job."

"She'd have a hard time cutting the lines on my bug," Gerald said. "They run pretty close to the frame."

"Why didn't you say so, Gerald?" Jack stood up and started for the door.

"I'll check my car, too," John said.

They all poured outside and immediately began inspecting the vehicles. There was a large puddle of gas under John and Gail's BMW. Heather's sports car had also been sabotaged. Everyone crowded around Gerald's bug as he finally picked himself up and dusted off after inspecting the underneath of his car. He looked up at them. "She cut my fuel lines, too."

"So we are stuck up here," John said grimly.

"Looks that way," Jack said.

Then Gerald added, "But she cut them in the wrong place. She couldn't cut them along the frames, so she followed them up to where the gas tank is...except in a VW

Beetle, the gas tank is in the front, not the back. I guess she didn't know that."

"So what are you saying, Gerald?" Heather asked, still not fully recovered from her ordeal with the dead deer.

"He's saying that the fuel didn't leak out," Jack said. "Right, Gerald?"

Gerald nodded. "Only partially. I can clamp some hosing around the broken lines. I'll just need to cut a few pieces from one of the other cars. That is if you want me to."

John clasped his hands together. "Gerald, my boy, you're a genius. By all means, go to it."

Gerald shuffled off and headed towards Heather's injured sports car. Heather looked after him with a quizzical look. Then she walked to him with a finger held up. "Um...excuse me...just what are you planning to do with my car?"

"I need to cut a few small hoses to fix my bug."

"Wait a minute," she protested, "why does it have to be *my* car?"

Gerald turned, not knowing what to say.

"Well?" Heather insisted.

Jack walked up. "You see, it's like this 'Miss Heather'...he could probably get the pieces he needs from my truck, but it's a ways down the road. That would mean he would have to walk all the way down there, work on it, then walk all the way up here and fix his car. He might even be able to get the pieces from John's BMW, but you know how expensive it is to fix cars like that. Yours is the logical choice."

"This is so unfair!" she said. "You people are...taking advantage of my poor car."

"Look," Jack said, sympathetically, "I said I would pay half to get your car fixed. I'll throw in the few extra bucks to fix your hoses. Okay?"

"Oh, that's mighty big of you, Jack," she retorted. "I probably won't ever see you again once we get out of this place."

"I may be a lot of things," Jack said, "but I'm not a liar.

I'll keep my word."

She turned on her heel and walked back to lean on the VW and pouted.

***

After some time, Gerald, having repaired his fuel lines, arose from his work. "Well, she should be as good as new. What's the plan, Jack?"

Jack rubbed his chin. "I was thinking you could drive me into town. We'll tell the local police what's going on."

"You're not leaving me here with that dead animal," Heather stated emphatically.

"I think it would be best that we each give our statement," John said. "It might help our credibility."

"I would also rather not stay behind," Gail agreed.

Jack looked at the bug, quite aware that the car was not known for having a spacious interior. He spoke to them all. "You do realize, don't you, that whoever leaves this place stands a big chance of missing out on their money? I mean, whoever's behind this clearly stated that we weren't supposed to leave before the week is up."

"I don't really care about that," Gail said. "My jewelry is worth much more than that. Don't you think so John?"

John Forrest grimaced. "Well, in sentimental value if nothing else," he said.

"What are we supposed to do, wait here and starve?" Heather asked.

Gerald opened the driver's door and paused. "How will they know we left, anyhow?"

"I don't know," Jack said. "I think the army woman ruled out any hidden bugs or cameras. Maybe if we get back in time, they won't even know we were gone."

"I get the front seat!" Heather exclaimed with girlish excitement. She pounced into the car and adjusted the mirror to her face. "God, my hair is a mess."

Gerald let John and Gail in before taking the driver's seat. Jack bent down to Heather, who was busy running her fingers through her hair. "Heather, normally I wouldn't really care who sits in front, but I would much rather you sit in back. It's going to be tight in the back regardless, but it'll be a lot less packed if you sit back there instead of me."

Heather narrowed her eyes at him. "Admit it, Jack. It's some sort of male ego thing to have the front seat, isn't it?"

"What? All I'm saying is..."

"Forget it, Jack, you're not getting your way this time," she said evenly.

Jack glanced to the back seat and was met with Gail's cold stare. She didn't say a word, but he knew instantly what she was communicating. She didn't want Heather sitting in the back seat with her and her husband at any price. He looked at John, who shrugged his shoulders and wore a tight smile.

"Uh...perhaps you're right," Jack said. "Would you at least move the back of your seat so I can get in?"

"Certainly," she said with a lady-like voice.

Jack pushed himself in, grabbing hold of the back of Gerald's seat and coming very close to the far window before finally settling in. Gail had to reposition herself so that she was almost sitting on her husband.

"Uh-oh," Gerald said in a worried tone.

"What's the matter? Let's go," Heather said.

Gerald paused and then looked nervously around at his cramped passengers. "I forgot about my starter."

Jack leaned forward. "What about your starter? The car works, doesn't it?"

"Yeah, but my starter's bad. I've got a new one, but I just haven't had the time to put it in yet."

"Do you mean to tell me," Gail said, "that we can't go anywhere until you change your starter?"

"Oh, no. No, we can go. It's just that someone's going to have to get out and push-start us."

"Oh, this is great," Jack said, leaning back in the seat, hitting John's shoulder. "Well, Heather, you wanted the front seat. Get out and push."

"Very funny. Even if I were strong enough, do you think

I'd endanger these nails?" She held up a perfect set of brightly painted red fingernails.

John rubbed his shoulder. "I wouldn't mind, but I know very little about cars. How does one go about 'push-starting'?"

"Oh, good grief," Jack said, exasperated. "Let me out, Heather."

Jack got out and easily pushed the car backward down the drive. It rolled away from him and Gerald steered it to the end of the drive. He turned it sharply so that it pointed towards the dirt road. Jack looked down the drive at the halted vehicle and spread his arms out. "Why didn't it start?"

Gerald stuck his head out of the window. "I don't think you can do that in reverse, can you? Just give me a push towards the road."

Jack shook his head and walked to the rear of the car. He started pushing, but the car slowed to a stop on the sandy dirt road. He grunted and groaned, barely budging it. "How-can-such-a-little-car-weigh-so-damn-much?"

He heard John's voice protrude from inside. "Perhaps we should get out. It might make it easier for you."

"No," Jack protested with a red face. "Just stay in the damn car. I don't want to do this twice."

The hot sun beat down upon his back and Jack could feel the sweat beginning to drip down his face. The car finally moved. He started to pick up momentum. The road was a little harder now and suddenly Gerald popped the clutch. The car bucked, the motor belched and the bug lurched forward once before it died. Jack let out a ferocious groan. He placed his hands carefully on the back hatch and tried to catch his breath.

"Is he going to push us again or what?" Heather asked Gerald.

Jack clenched his teeth and spoke slowly and carefully. "This time, Gerald, when I get the car moving, *wait* until I say 'now' before you let that clutch out. Okay?"

"Okay, Jack."

The car was a little easier to start rolling this time. Jack huffed and puffed behind it, picking up speed. Finally, when he was nearing a jogging pace, he called to Gerald. "Now!"

Gerald popped the clutch again and the bug lurched forward. Almost instantly, the engine came to life, sputtering and spitting into normal operation. He put the car in neutral and waited for Jack to catch up. Heather pulled her seat forward. "I knew you were good for something," she said.

As Jack tried to situate himself, John said, "That was really quite interesting. I had no idea you could start a car in such a way. It's good information to have. Say, perhaps, if my starter malfunctions in the middle of nowhere and my cell phone is out of range. I could, hypothetically speaking, get my car going again."

Jack wiped his forehead. "Does your car have an automatic transmission?"

"Of course. What does that have to do with it?"

Jack sighed. "I'd just like to be there when you tried to push-start it."

Heather's perky nose dabbed at the air and finally identified the source of its discomfort. "God, Jack, you smell."

Jack brought his hands out in front of him, stiffening them to the size stranglehold that would fit around Heather's neck. As he began reaching towards the passenger in front of him, John put his arm out. "Believe me, I know how you feel. But you must rise above it."

"If he doesn't do it, I will," Gail said passively as she gazed out the window.

CHAPTER TWELVE

Thirty miles later, the puke-green bug sputtered into the small town of Bunky. The town itself was little more than a spot in the road. The buildings were edged up alongside the main highway as if they were all eager to take advantage of the sparse passing traffic. Further down, more buildings could be seen, the spaces between them growing larger as the road stretched on. Very few vehicles could be seen and only an occasional pedestrian emerged from a shop or traveled down the sidewalk. The two-story brick buildings dated the city to the early fifties, with barely any hint of modernization.

"They probably don't even have a police station here," Heather noted, dismissing any importance of the town with the tone of her voice.

"There it is," Gail said. "See it Gerald?

"Yeah, but isn't that a barber shop sign?"

An outdated squad car was parked along the curb. The building in front of it had a large sign that read: 'Sheriff's Office'. Near the front door was an old-style red and white twirling barbershop sign. A large window boasted 'Ed's Barber Shop' and someone was getting a trim inside.

Jack said, "Just try to back in somewhere so it will be easier to push start this thing later."

Gerald settled the bug on the other side of the street and

they all climbed out. Jack surveyed the town from this closer perspective. A few of the buildings had benches in front of them. An old man sat reading a newspaper across the street. Some of the shop owners could be seen through the large windows of their stores. There was nobody blatantly staring, but Jack couldn't help but feel that the whole town had their collective eyes on them.

Gerald looked slowly around, following Jack's survey. "I've seen Twilight Zone episodes that looked like this."

"Yeah," Jack agreed.

John finished stretching from his cooped-up ride. "Well," he said, "shall we report our injustice?"

"You guys go ahead," Gerald said, "I'm going to fix my starter. I'll probably have it done by the time you come back."

"Alright," Jack said, "let's see what we can do."

They walked across the street, noticing that the main street was composed of neatly placed brick like the streets of yesteryear. The door to the Sheriff's office was made of heavy, antique wood with a nicely shaped brass handle. They opened it and went in. Inside there was a tall, thin man cutting hair on the left side of the room. He nodded to them upon their entrance and continued his work. The right side of the room contained a few filing cabinets, an oak desk, and a small rotating fan.

"Excuse me," Jack said to the barber. "Are we in the right place? We're looking for the Sheriff's office."

The barber looked up again. When he spoke, his rotten green teeth could be seen. "You got the right place," he said in a hoarse voice. "Sheriff's here. He's in the back. I'm sure he'll be out in a minute."

"Thanks," Jack said, noticing the man in the barber's seat for the first time. He was very large with a round face. The man had a crew cut, but that didn't stop the barber from continuing his work.

Gail tapped Jack lightly on the shoulder and spoke in a low voice, "I don't know about this Jack, maybe we should ..."

Gail was interrupted by the sound of the back door opening up. A tall man in a tan Sheriff's uniform entered the office holding a mug of coffee. His hair was jet-black, cleanly cut and his features were sharply chiseled upon his face. High cheekbones hinted a Native American heritage. His dark eyes appeared to be both fierce and honest. His muscular frame filled out the neatly pressed uniform well, sending a message of strong authority behind the Silver Star he wore.

The Sheriff placed the coffee mug on a free space on the desk while looking up and taking in the sight of his visitors. His expression seemed to be on the brink of impatience. "Can I help you folks?"

Heather had watched the man intently from the moment he entered, trying to find a flaw in his appearance. Until now, she was completely convinced that this town didn't have anything to offer. When the Sheriff looked at them with his dark, honest eyes, a small sound escaped from her that was somewhere between a sigh and a gasp. She started to answer his question when Jack spoke up. Heather glared at Jack, but the expression went unnoticed.

"I hope so, Sheriff. My name is Jack Eastman." He gestured towards the others. "This is John Forest and his wife, Gail and -"

"My name is Heather DuMorrier, Sheriff." She nodded slightly, wearing her 'I'm delighted to meet you' face.

The Sheriff's expression did not waver. "I'm Sheriff Clay. What can I do for you?"

"Sheriff," Jack said, "if you don't mind, we'd like to sit down. This may take a few minutes."

The Sheriff gestured to the gray chairs that were on the other side of his desk. They sat down and Jack paused for a moment, trying to decide where to start. Finally, he said, "This may sound a little strange, but..."

***

Gerald removed the first starter bolt and was struggling with the second one when something big blocked out the sun. He squinted up at a human eclipse. It was a very big man with a beard and Gerald saw Paul standing before him. He jumped slightly, dropped his wrench and it went clanging to the ground.

"Sixty-seven?" The man asked.

"Huh?" Gerald replayed the man's voice in his mind. Definitely not Paul.

"Your bug. Is it a sixty-seven?"

"Oh. Yeah, it is. You must really know your VW's."

"I used to be into them. I'm a mechanic, too. You get to know a bit about the different models. Looks like you got yourself a hobby car."

"Yeah," Gerald agreed. "I'm going to completely restore it someday."

The man gestured toward the starter. "You need some help with that?"

"Uh, no thanks. I've got it under control."

"Well, I'm just down the street at Joe's Garage if you need a hand. My name's Joe."

"I'm Gerald." Gerald stuck out a greasy hand and was met by one of similar texture.

"Well, Gerald, I'm going to leave you to your work. I need to grab a bite to eat before I get back to the grind."

Food. Suddenly, Gerald realized just how hungry he was. "Where do you go to get a good meal in this town?"

Joe pointed down the walkway in the direction he was heading. "Betsy's Kitchen. You won't find anything like it for miles."

Gerald gave the man a wave and said, "Thanks". Continuing with his work, he began talking to himself. "First Ed's Barber Shop, then Joe's Garage and now Betsy's Kitchen." He grunted while he loosened the starter from its mounting bracket. "Definitely Twilight Zone."

***

"Let me get this straight," the Sheriff said. "Someone is paying you all to live together up there in that summer home?"

"Yeah," Jack said, "but the point is this woman that was with us —"

"The one dressed in fatigues," the Sheriff said, trying to follow the story.

"Yeah, that one. She stole everything of value that we had. The big guy, Paul, caught her. Then he decided that *he* would run off with our stolen items. He took the woman hostage and left."

"He had a gun," Heather said. "He pointed it right at her head. I wouldn't have believed Polecat would do anything like that."

The Sheriff cocked his head. "Polecat?"

"That's what he goes by," Jack said. "We don't know what his last name is."

By now, another customer had entered the barbershop across the room and was in the middle of a trim. He was older than the barber and a mop of pure white hair covered his head. He called out from his red-striped barber's chair. "Polecat. Now that sounds like a shady character to me if ever there was one." The old man laughed.

The Sheriff ignored the intrusion. "And the woman he was with? What was her name?"

"Well, she wasn't exactly the social type," John said. "We didn't have the opportunity to get her name."

Sheriff Clay leaned on his desk. "You people were living together and you don't know their names?"

The man in the barber's chair called out again. "That's how people are these days, Sheriff. Nobody really talks to each other anymore."

"Does he have to do that?" Jack asked.

The Sheriff spoke to the old man without turning his head. "Monty, could you please not interrupt what I'm doing here?"

The old man waved a disappointed hand in acknowledgment.

"Could I ask," Jack said, "why you have a barber shop in your office?"

"We share the building. It goes back to the history of two co-owners who had a dispute settled by the town mayor. It's part of our town history, but I don't have time to go into it right now. You were saying you didn't know their names?"

"She was pretty strange," Gail said, trying to invoke a tone of reason. "We thought it best to keep our distance from her."

"What was this man driving when he left?"

"Well, he started out in my truck," Jack said, "but the woman cut all our fuel lines. He got a little ways down the road when the truck stopped. Then he found a motorcycle in the bushes. We think it was originally going to be her getaway, but Paul took off with it, carrying the army women with him. It was a Harley-Davidson with shiny chrome and a good paint job. It looked new from what I could see."

The Sheriff sighed. "Well, that's some story."

Heather blinked up at him. "Is there any way you can help us, Sheriff? You just can't imagine what we've been through. We've had the power go out, our lives threatened by that insane woman, my car is wrecked, the flooding in the basement..." Her voice began to quiver. "That horrid dead animal..."

"Okay, ma'am, just calm down. I'll do everything I can. They could be miles away by now, though. There's no guarantee they came this way, either. I'm going to need as much description from each of you as possible. I'll alert the state police. From the sound of that Harley, it should stick out like a sore thumb around these parts. It doesn't sound like this guy had any big plans to do this, so he probably hasn't put much thought into what he's doing. Most likely, he'll screw up along the way and when he does, I'll be there."

"Oh, thank you," Heather said, wiping away an invisible tear. "You know, when I first saw you, I knew you were a man of action. If anyone can get these crooks, I believe it will be you."

Jack resisted the overwhelming urge to roll his eyes.

CHAPTER THIRTEEN

Garby William Johnson looked pensively again at the vehicles in front of the house. "You sure you didn't see anybody inside?"

Garby's best friend and accomplice, Zack Tiller put his hand on the other boy's shoulder. "I'm telling ya, man, there ain't nobody in there. The place is deserted."

"Alright," Garby said. He lifted his tire iron again and put the wedge into the side of the front door. He struggled with it. The bright sunlight caught the fifteen year old's pale face and made an even sharper definition of his features. His long face seemed to curve forward, thrusting his chin to a point. His sinister eyes were revealed by two rectangular openings that rarely blinked. His nose was sharp but small like his mouth. Greasy blond hair matted straight down over his head and covered his ears.

Zack was evidently cut from a different mold. The boy's face was round and impregnated with pimples. His eyes were round, too, giving the impression of perpetual surprise. He had a little more meat on his bones than his skinny friend, but that may have been because he was a little shorter. His hair was brown and slightly curly and he had a habit of clenching his teeth.

"Man, this door must be made out of titanium," Garby said, taking a rest.

"We could try the back door," Zack said, reaching for the doorknob. He turned it and, to his surprise, the door opened.

"What the...?" Garby let the tire iron fall to the ground.

Zack grinned, revealing his perfectly mated teeth. "You just don't have the touch, man. You gotta have the touch."

They walked in.

"Whoa, look at this place," Zack said.

"Yeah, looks like somebody has some money."

"Oh, how untidy," Zack said, mocking a proper voice. "Somebody busted a vase all over the floor."

"I'm going to look upstairs, you check out the basement," Garby said.

"No way, man, you check out the basement."

"What, you chicken?"

"I just don't like basements, that's all," Zack protested.

"Well, get over it. Who knows, maybe there's money down there."

"Yeah, right. And maybe there's dead bodies down there."

Garby started flapping his arms and making chicken noises.

Zack rolled his eyes. "Just shut up." He headed for the basement door.

Within moments, Garby had looked through all the upstairs rooms and started his way back down the stairs. He noticed his friend looking around in the living room. "Find any dead bodies in the basement?"

Zack looked up at him. "No, but man do they have water problems."

Garby tapped the wall where he stood on the stairs. "Zack, my tool please."

Zack went outside, picked up the tire iron and brought it up to his friend. Garby said, "I think it's time we inspected the quality of this construction."

He tapped the tire iron lightly on the wall as if trying to find a hollow area. Then he swung the metal sharply, forcing a big hole in the wall. He slammed the wall several times, creating dents and holes in the sheet rock. He began letting out a yell as he swung. Then he turned to the rungs of the stairwell. He swung at them, cracking wood and knocking pieces loose in the process. Zack picked up one of the loose rungs. He slammed it into his hand and smiled with sinister pleasure. It was high-quality wood.

Zack went into the kitchen and began swinging the wood into the cabinets, smashing dishes, and glass. He clambered up on top of the kitchen table and jumped up and down until his weight cracked the table in half. Garby was working the living room now. He was hacking into the fireplace like a lumberjack. Bits of stone came flying off and then he brought the iron upward into the mantel. It split easily and Garby ripped at it until it lay in pieces on the floor. He stopped for a second to take a look at his work. Then, turning to the windows, he smiled a crooked smile. He ran towards the nearest window like a wild man charging for victory. He swung the iron into it as if swinging a baseball bat. As the glass flew, he swung in all directions, obliterating the opening. He took out another one, then another. Then he stopped. The constant noises of Zack's destruction were no longer in the background. He listened but didn't hear anything.

He called out tentatively, "Zack?"

Zack appeared from the hallway with a devilish grin. "Guess what I found?" He held three cans of bright orange aerosol paint in his hands.

"Oh, man," Garby laughed with delight, "bring it on!"

The two boys ran around the house spraying graffiti and orange streaks everywhere. When at last the paint had been depleted, they stood in the middle of the living room and surveyed the destruction.

Zack said, "Well, man, how does the quality rate?"

"I've seen better," Garby muttered. He gathered the empty paint cans under his arm and slid his iron through a belt loop.

"What are you gonna do with the cans?"

"You idiot. You want them to get our fingerprints? C'mon, get your piece of wood. Let's get outta here."

As they walked out, Zack said, "You know what? You won't believe it, man. There was a dead deer out on the back deck."

"No way. I wonder where it came from."

"I don't know, but I made sure it was dead."

"What do you mean?"

"Let's just say that not all of it is on the deck anymore."

Garby stopped in front of Heather's sports car. "Man, what happened to this thing."

"Yeah, looks like it would've been a pretty nice ride if it wasn't for this hood being all messed up."

Garby grinned and turned to his friend. "One more for the road?"

Zack looked at his friend with a gritty smile.

Garby set the paint cans down and the two circled the car like a couple of vultures before they began beating on it. They smashed the windows first, then put huge dents in the sides. Garby plowed the iron into a rear tire a few times until it was clear he couldn't make a hole in it without his tool bouncing off. He got mad at it, kicked the tire and started smashing the taillights. The two were in a frenzy now, bashing in the roof and busting the grillwork. Garby tried ripping at the tires again with no success. Finally, mad and nearly exhausted, he picked up the cans and motioned for his friend to follow him. They disappeared into the woods the way they had come.

***

The rushing water of the nearby stream put a constant pressure on the water wheel and to the dead limb that kept it from turning. A small crack, created when the limb first stopped the wheel, began to grow under the pressure. The limb creaked slightly as the water rushed into and past the wheel. Then there was a loud crack when the limb finally gave way. The wheel turned a little and then hesitated as part of the limb braced itself between the bottom of the stream and the wheel. The strong current forced the wheel to keep moving and the limb was pushed through the mud. Once free, the limb floated off and the wheel began turning at full speed once again.

CHAPTER FOURTEEN

At Betsy's diner, five strangers sat down at a round table while a waitress hovered over them and passed out menus. They could still feel the eyes of others upon them. Looking up to confront the source meant seeing a head-turning casually away. Other times, the person staring would continue to stare, almost like they couldn't comprehend strangers. Jack's eyes met with one man who seemed like he might be a truck driver. It was likely since the back of Betsy's diner contained a large parking lot where semi trucks frequented. The man did not look away and Jack wondered how people could be so rude to stare.

"Something's not right with that Sheriff," Jack said.

"Something's not right with this town," Gerald said, looking discreetly around.

Gail said, "What do you mean, Jack?"

"I mean something wasn't right. I don't know. It was like he was concerned about what we were saying, but for his own reasons."

"You're impossible, Jack," Heather said. "Just because we find someone that might actually accomplish something, your masculinity is threatened."

"Yeah, that must be it," Jack said, sarcastically. Then he turned to the others and continued. "He seemed somehow familiar also. I can't quite put my finger on it, but it seems like I've seen him somewhere before."

"Yes," John said slowly. "I know what you mean. He does seem somewhat familiar now that you mention it."

As her husband spoke, Gail's eyes widened and she pointed silently across the room. They all turned to look as she said, "Is that who I think it is?"

John squinted. "I don't have my glasses on. Who is it?"

She answered in a hushed voice. "Is that him? Is that Polecat?"

Gerald turned back to the table and waved the possibility away. "No, that's not Polecat. That's Joe. I met him while I was working on the car. He runs a garage up the road. I thought it was him too when I first saw him."

"Well he certainly looks a lot like him," Gail said.

"He sure does in a way," Jack agreed.

"You guys are crazy," Heather said. "He looks nothing like Polecat.

The waitress returned with some drinks, took their order and disappeared again. Jack took a sip of his coffee with his eyes still on the big man. He sat his mug down. "I'll be right back," he announced.

Heather hissed at him. "Jack, don't make a fool out of yourself, sit back down. Leave that man alone."

Jack walked across the room to the booth that Joe was sitting in. This close, the resemblance was superficial. The man was big. He had a scraggly beard. Other than that, the similarities were few. This man was older with a lot of gray working its way into his beard. He wore round glasses as he read his newspaper and he seemed to have an air of intelligence about him. Jack nearly stopped, questioning whether he should interrupt the man's meal. It could be nothing. Then he found himself in front of the man's booth. The man looked up at him. The eyes. Was there a similarity?

"Hello, uh Joe?" Jack said, feeling awkward. "Sorry to bother you. My name's Jack. I think you've met a friend of mine. Gerald with the VW..."

The man came to life. "Oh, yeah. Yeah, the kid out

front with a car. Sure, what can I do for you?"

"Well, I was wondering if I could talk to you for a minute if you don't mine."

Joe shrugged his shoulders. "Have a seat. Does he need me to help him with his car or something?"

"No. I think he's got it fixed. Actually, I was wondering if you might know somebody by the name of Paul. He goes by the nickname of Polecat."

Joe chuckled and nodded his head. Jack was startled by the similarity to Paul's trademark chuckle. "You know him?"

"Hell, yeah, I know 'em," Joe said. "He's my brother."

Jack started. "Your brother? Is that right?"

"Yeah, that's right. That is when I claim him. What has he done now?"

Jack felt a quick wave of self-satisfaction wash over him. He had played a hunch and was right. It just might be possible to get their belongings back after all.

"I really don't know how to tell you this, Joe, but your brother robbed me and my friends."

Joe squinted through his glasses. "What'd you say?"

"Actually, we were being robbed by someone else. It's kind of a long story, but he caught this other person ripping us off. At first, I don't think he had any intention of doing us wrong. Once he had our belongings in his hands, though...I don't know. It was like a sudden change came over him. I guess he suddenly got the idea that he could get away with our valuables. Then, he took off with the original thief as a hostage. Joe, I don't think me or any of my friends want to put him in jail. We just want our belongings back."

"That damn idiot," Joe muttered.

"Excuse me?"

"My brother," Joe explained, "doesn't have a lot upstairs if you know what I mean. He doesn't mean any harm, but sometimes the line between right and wrong is a little blurry to him. If he gets a notion, don't matter what it is, he runs with it. He gets in more trouble that way."

Jack grimaced. "I'm afraid we've already spoken to the

Sheriff about this. It was the first thing we wanted to do when we got into town."

"Oh, that's okay," Joe said. "Sheriff's used to it by now."

Jack looked perplexed. "Are you saying that the Sheriff knows Polecat?"

"Oh, yeah. He knows him more than he'd like to admit. The Sheriff's pretty easy on him. He threw him in jail a few times, but it doesn't do much good. He spent the night in a cell for drunk and disorderly one time and for hunting deer out of season another. My brother's bullheaded, as bullheaded as they come. He's gonna do things his way no matter what."

"I see," Jack said, taking it all in. "Do you have any idea where we might find him?"

"Nope. He could be anywhere. That explains why he hasn't been to work these past few days. Hell, I just got through rebuilding an engine all by myself. I'd fire his ass if he wasn't my brother." Joe leaned forward a little. "If you find him, you tell him to get his butt back to work. I'm tired of doing all of it myself."

"Yeah," Jack said, rising from the booth, "I sure will. If he comes back..."

"If I see him first," Joe said, "I'll get your stuff back, don't you worry about that."

"I appreciate it, Joe. Like I said, I don't think he meant to do us any harm."

"Yeah, he never does," Joe sighed. "Good luck in finding him."

Jack strolled back to the table where the others were already digging into the newly arrived food. "Well, you aren't going to believe this," he said.

CHAPTER FIFTEEN

Fifteen miles out of town, Paul parked the motorcycle under a big shade tree just off the main highway. A few hills created by a nearby quarry construction jutted up from the otherwise desolate landscape. After setting the bike on its kickstand, Paul backed up and admired it again in this new peaceful setting. "Where'd you get this thing anyway? I don't ever remember seeing this beauty around town."

The army woman was still sitting on the bike, glaring at her abductor. She jumped off and slapped Paul across his head. "You idiot! What on earth did you think you were trying to prove?"

Paul chuckled and made an ill attempt at fixing his scraggly hair. "C'mon now, Kola, you and me can share this loot. No need for you to keep it all to yourself. Or maybe I should tell your big brother about it."

"Go ahead. When I tell him what really happened, he'll throw you in jail."

Paul eyed her sharply. "You mean when you *lie* about what really happened."

"Who do you think he will believe? Me or you?"

"Listen, I'm the one who's got the stuff." He held up the backpack. "I'll split it with you, but I'm not going to just give it back."

"No need to," she said, crossing her arms. "Just keep it."

Paul eyed her suspiciously. "What do you mean?"

"Just keep it. I'll go tell Dennis and then he'll have a really good reason to throw you in jail."

"I'll go tell Dennis," Paul mocked her. "I'll go tell my big brother, the sheriff who always gets me out of trouble every time I get myself in a little jam."

"You're one to talk," she retorted. "How many times have I seen your brother pull you out of the bar just before you got your butt kicked?"

"Forget it then," Paul said. "I'll pawn it myself. Too bad you worked so hard and now you ain't gonna get to keep any of it."

"Listen to me, you ugly skunk," she said. "If you don't give it back to me, I'll see how much of this clay around here I can shove down your throat!"

Paul chuckled. "You ain't changed since grade school, woman. All talk and no action. I don't care if you did spend a couple of years in the military. I remember when you was a little girl. Yeah, I remember when they gave you yer name. Remember that? Remember back when that soda store was right next to Ed's? Man, I can see it just like yesterday. I was sittin' in a booth slurping down one of those big strawberry shakes they used to make. You were sittin' up there with your daddy, 'ol mayor Clay. You was maybe seven at the most. I looked over just in time to see you pull your soda across the counter. The dang thing was about as big as you were. You spilt it all over your new dress. Drenched in Coca-Cola. Man, you cried and cried."

"Shut up with the history and give me my bag."

"No, wait a minute," Paul continued. "I think there's something you don't know. You don't know who it was that told everybody in school about that little incident. From then on, it was no more Kayla Clay. That name kinda stuck didn't it, Kola? Or should I call you 'army woman'? That had to be eating you up, having been in the marines and all."

"You mean to tell me you're the idiot moron that spread that story?"

"What's the matter? Don't like the name I gave you?"

Kola stared at the ground for a moment, looking like she was ready to spit bullets. Then she let out a yell of rage and swung around with a high kick. Her karate kick struck Paul on the side of the head and bent him over sideways. Dazed, he had no time to recover before the next kick caught him between the legs. He doubled over, letting the backpack go and fell against the bike, knocking it to the ground with him. He groaned in pain as she casually walked over and picked up her bag. She dusted it off and looked at him. "You probably don't have the slightest idea where the nickname 'Polecat' came from, do you, you stinking moron?"

Paul grunted as he rolled over and snatched up his rifle. He was quick, but she was already running towards the construction mine. He yelled after her in anger. "Woman, you're gonna wish you never kicked nobody."

***

Jack and the others left Betsy's diner feeling like they had eaten two days' worth of food. They walked towards Gerald's car, not quite sure what to do next. They stopped upon hearing a strange sound come from the corner of the building. Looking over to the corner, they caught a glimpse of an old man beckoning to them. "Over here," he whispered, "just one of you."

Jack, perplexed, motioned for the others to stay behind as he walked over to the corner. Around the edge was the old man from the barbershop, the one who kept interrupting. He had a worried look in his old wrinkled eyes as he spoke. "C'mon over here, I don't want Sheriff Clay to see me."

Jack moved further into the alley that separated two buildings. When the old man thought it was safe, he spoke again in a hushed voice. "I shouldn't say anything. I should be minding my own business is what I should be doing."

"Look," Jack said, "if you know something that will help us..."

"That motorbike you're looking for, I've seen it before. It went past here earlier. Looked like they were heading right out of town. That big boy that works over at Joe's, he was driving it. And it looked like the Sheriff's sister was with him."

"The Sheriff's sister?" Jack's eyes narrowed and then realization crept into his expression. No wonder the Sheriff seemed so familiar.

"I don't know where they were headed. Nothing out there except an old quarry mine about fifteen miles out. Hey, don't tell Sheriff Clay I told you all this."

"Don't worry," Jack said, clasping his hand on the man's shoulder. "Thanks for your help." He was about to turn and leave when the old man nudged him with an outstretched hand.

"Huh? Oh. Look, we don't have much money…"

The man's eyes beckoned him as if it would be an insult if he didn't receive compensation for his information. Jack hurriedly gave the old man several bills. The old man nodded his head and disappeared down the alley.

The others stood near the car, puzzled. When Jack returned he said, "I think we have a lead as to where Paul went. Gerald, let's take a ride and see if we can find out where he's hiding. John, will you and Gail snoop around and see if you can find out any information about who owns that house we've been staying in?"

"Yes, of course," John said, "it's about time we get to the bottom of this."

"What about me," Heather asked. "What should I do?"

Jack was getting into the car. "Stay in town and try to keep out of trouble."

"No way, Jack, I'm coming with you. I'm going to give Polecat a piece of my mind."

"It's not a good idea, Heather. It could get dangerous," Jack said, hoping to sway her from an argument.

"Wait a minute," Heather said, suddenly excited. "I know what I can do. I'll find Sheriff Clay so he can help us."

This gave Jack pause. "Uh, yeah, that's a good idea, Heather, but it looks like as if he's already gone. Why don't you go ahead and join us and maybe we'll run into him."

"Are you sure? What if he comes back while we're gone?"

"He's probably headed the same way we are," Jack said, getting out of the front seat and moving to the back. "We're sure to run into him. Besides, we might just need your help after all."

"Why, Jack," Heather said, sliding into the front seat, "that's the most intelligent thing you've said all week. I'll be glad to help. See, things aren't so hard when you treat a person the right way."

Jack wearily said, "Straight on out of town, Gerald."

CHAPTER SIXTEEN

Paul peeked around the edge of a large conveyor machine. The place was filled with machinery dedicated to the processing of minerals from the quarry. A lot of people from town worked here. He remembered when he used to work out here. He had the job exactly two days before they fired him for insubordination. Paul went on break thirty minutes early and his supervisor later told him that he could only go at his appointed time. Paul told the supervisor where to go and a big argument ensued. It was the only job Paul ever had besides working for his brother.

Paul looked up at one of the large storage buildings. He called out, "You might as well come out now, Kola. I may not be the best fighter in the world, but I can track anything. I can smell ya, girl. If I have to come in after you, I might be tempted to use this here gun."

A silence followed as he listened intently. Then he heard something fall. He thought it must have been a heavy piece of metal because it clanged loudly before and a smile grew across Paul's face. "You ain't as smart as you thought you was," he muttered to himself and started moving to the building.

***

"They were definitely here," Gerald said, pulling the beetle up to where the motorcycle lay in the sand.

They got out of the car and Jack walked over to the motorcycle, examining the nearby ground. "Looks like they had a fight," he said.

"How can you tell that?" Heather asked.

"Easy," Jack explained. "Look at all these footprints in this one area. And the bike was knocked off its kickstand somehow. Something big must have hit it to knock it over."

"Polecat?" Gerald offered.

"I would say so. Tracks leading off towards that mining company. One could be chasing the other."

"I think we should go get Sheriff Clay," Heather said. "We can't handle this by ourselves."

"Not a good idea, Heather," Jack said. "They could be long gone by the time we find the Sheriff. Besides, I have a feeling the Sheriff wouldn't be much help anyway."

Heather stopped and stared at Jack. "Is this some kind of macho crap you're trying to pull? What do you mean he wouldn't be much help? He's the Sheriff; it's his job. What if Polecat shoots at us or that crazy woman attacks us? We need to find the Sheriff and let him deal with this."

"Listen, Heather. The Sheriff isn't--"

It was then that they heard the loud clanging sound of metal off in the distance towards the mining area.

Jack surveyed the area more closely and turned to Gerald. "See if you can go around to the right. I'll follow the perimeter around to the left. We'll meet up behind the plant out where that big building is. One of us should be able to see something along the way. Then, we'll decide what to do."

Gerald nodded his head uneasily and then started walking.

"No way, Jack," Heather protested. "This is a ridiculous idea."

"Maybe," Jack said, walking away, "but it's a plan. Either come with me or stay out of sight somewhere."

Heather groaned in exasperation as she watched the two of them walk off in different directions. Finally, she started after Jack, her high heels sinking down as she walked over the orange clay.

***

"Madam, I know something about real estate," John was saying. "And I know something about public record. We have a right to see what we ask for and if you would be so kind to let us examine the records, then we will be on our way."

An old woman sat on a high chair behind the counter at the Clerk of the County Court office. She squinted up at him with horn-rimmed spectacles. Her face was etched with deep wrinkles that branched out from where her lips should have been. "Listen to me, young man," she said, "I've been working here for the past thirty years and I know what you can and can't look at."

John started to speak up again but sighed instead. Gail, sensing her husband's aggravation, put a hand on his arm and turned to the woman. "We're very interested in purchasing some land nearby. We need to get an idea of the type of parcels that are in the surrounding area. It won't take but a few moments of your time."

"There ain't any land for sale in that area," the woman ranted. "I know you're just trying to hop onto some land that's piling up back-taxes. Well, there ain't any of those, either, so you can forget it."

John looked blankly at the wall for a moment. Then, a feeling of illumination came over him. He turned back to the old woman with an apologetic expression. "I'm sorry, we should have told you the truth from the beginning," he began.

Gail looked at him in bewilderment.

"You see, we are not from around here. Well, I guess you realize that. My wife and I have been working on a project for quite some time now. We have become very interested in learning about our family history, our genealogy. We have traced my great-grandfather's line to this town and I have reason to believe that he once owned a house in this area. I'm not really concerned with financial figures or parcel sizes, but rather the names of people who have owned property here in the past."

"Well, why didn't you say so in the first place," the woman said in a mocking voice. "I mean, if you're looking for family, that's different." Then she leaned forward and said in a sweet, grandmotherly type voice, "The Public Library is three blocks down the street."

***

"Jack," Heather hissed, "will you wait up?"

Jack stopped, exasperated. "Can't you move any faster?"

"My high heels are getting stuck in this clay," she complained. She looked at her shoes. "They're getting ruined. This is all your fault, Jack. You can add the cost of these shoes to what you owe me on the car. They aren't cheap, either."

Jack sighed. "Can you shut up for just one minute? Do you want them to know where we are before we know where they are?"

Heather glared at him. "You ought to try walking in these things."

Jack rubbed his chin and looked at her shoes. "I can see your point," he said. "Mind if I take a look at them for a minute."

"What? Why?"

"Well, to tell you the truth, it has always amazed me how women walk in those things. May I?"

"Jack, you're wasting time," she said, slipping her shoes off and handing them to him. "They're going to get away with this all because you have a shoe fetish."

Jack immediately broke off the spiked heels and threw them aside as Heather gasped.

She said, "Do you have any idea how much those shoes cost?"

"It doesn't matter," Jack said. "I just improved their value. More comfortable and more practical. Now, let's keep moving."

Fuming, she put the shoes back on and walked after him. "Jack, you are the most irritating, rude, inconsiderate son of a --"

They immediately fell into a large hole. Heather screamed on the way down. It was deep. A flash of fear went through Jack's mind as he had visions of falling into an extremely deep well. That was just before he and Heather hit the ground about fifteen feet from the surface.

CHAPTER SEVENTEEN

"It was a valiant attempt, dear," Gail said as she and her husband moved along the sidewalk.

"Old biddy. This backward town does not know one thing about the meaning of public records. It means they are open to the public. It is like they are still living in the forties. Perhaps even further back than that."

"I know," Gail agreed. "Don't worry about it. We simply have to find another way."

"Well, what she said about the library really isn't a bad idea. That is, as long as they don't keep their books under lock and key."

Gail stopped. "You know something, dear? I feel like a mystery sleuth working on a fascinating case. This is actually quite fun."

"Yes, quite," John agreed, seeing it from her perspective. "The others ought to really appreciate the trouble we are going through."

***

Heather winced as she tried to straighten her leg out from under her body. Then she cried out when she felt how painful it was. Jack coughed from the dust they created in the fall. He pushed his hands into the small of his back and cracked something back into place. The light from above illuminated the space a little. They were at the bottom of a hole about six feet in diameter.

"Are you okay?" Jack asked.

"I don't know. I think I've broken something," Heather said moaned.

"Where do you hurt?"

"My right leg. I can't get it out from under me."

They were somewhat tangled. When Jack hit the bottom, Heather came directly after and slid off his shoulder. One leg was over his and his arm ended up being pinned by her back. With some effort, he straightened and slowly stood up.

"Let me lift you up," Jack said. "Then we can take a look at it."

"I don't know, Jack. It hurts." Before she knew what was happening, he was lifting her up. She was surprised at how easily he did it. Then, as her leg straightened out, she felt waves of pain and tears pushed their way out of her eyes. "Ow, ow, ow," she cried, "it hurts, it hurts."

"Okay, okay," Jack said, easing her back down to the ground. He sat her up against the outside wall so her legs would stretch out as much as possible. "Alright, let's see how bad it is."

"Don't touch it!"

"Calm down, we need to find out if it's broken."

"It hurts."

"I know. I'll be careful." He moved his hands cautiously onto the swollen area, taking care when the pain seized her. He couldn't help but to notice how nice her legs looked. He had noticed before when he first met her, but that pleasantry was quickly erased when she started blaming him for wrecking her car.

"Ouch!" She yelled. Like a quick reflex, she lifted her other leg and kicked him in the chest, knocking him hard against the wall. Luckily, her heels were no longer on her feet.

"What are you doing?" Jack growled. "Do you think I

feel perfectly fine after falling in this hell hole? Ever stop to think my ribs might be broken?"

"You hurt me," she squealed then added, "You don't have any broken ribs."

"I might as well have. You know, I've had nothing but pain since I've met you. You blame me for wrecking your car, nearly drown me and kick me down a flight of stairs. And now this. I should have left you back with John and Gail."

"I don't think they wanted me with them anyway," Heather said, nearly sobbing. "It's broken. I need a doctor."

"It's not broken, but it is sprained pretty badly. We need to get you some medical attention."

"How do you know it's not broken? You're not a doctor."

"No, I'm not a doctor. But I know it's not broken. Just try not to move it."

"Yeah," she laughed sarcastically, "there's plenty of room to move around in here."

Jack cupped his hands to his mouth and called out. "Gerald!"

"Shut up," she hissed, "Do you want them to find us?"

"Heather, at this point I really don't care. I think I'd rather be shot than to be stuck down here with you."

***

Gerald made his way around the perimeter to the back of the large building. He took in the view, squinting in the sunlight. There was nothing to the left where he had come from, but to the right he could see most of the processing machinery. Jack and Heather were not in sight.

"C'mon you guys," he said quietly, "where are you?"

Suddenly, another loud clanging noise came from the building. Cautiously, Gerald moved closer to a rear door. To his surprise, it was unlocked. He slowly opened it and slipped inside.

The inside of the building was like a smaller version of

some of the machinery outside though it was huge in its own right. Vast conveyor belts climbed upward to a giant central funnel. Some twenty feet below the funnel was a row of large containers that sat on rails. The rails spiraled around the floor and vanished under a large roll-up door to the outside. The container that sat directly under the funnel was loaded with the orange clay-like substance from the quarry. Out of the corner of his eye, Gerald saw a movement on the far side of the building. Instinctively, he hid himself behind a nearby forklift. He looked again, this time focusing in on the image of Paul walking inside the building. He had his rifle in one hand and carelessly banged the barrel against the machinery that he passed. The sound echoed throughout the building and Gerald felt his heart thumping.

"Kol-laa," Paul coaxed, "come out, come out wherever you are."

"What took you so long?" Her voice echoed. It was impossible to tell where the sound came from.

Paul immediately raised the gun and pointed it desperately in different directions. "Come out, woman. I'm still willin' to split it fifty-fifty."

"I'm afraid it's not going to be that easy," came her voice.

There was the sound of a few clangs and then someone running over grated metal. Again, Paul whisked the gun around, trying to ascertain the direction of the sound. "Play yer games, woman," Paul said to himself, "but when I'm done with ya, yer gonna wish you never tangled with me."

CHAPTER EIGHTEEN

Heather looked up at Jack nervously. "What are you doing?"

"I'm just going to see if I can climb out and find out what's going on out there."

"No, Jack," Heather begged, "please don't leave me alone down here."

"I'll be right back. I promise."

"No!" There was desperation to her voice that startled Jack and caused him to sit slowly back down. She said, "I...I can't handle being down here alone."

"Alright," Jack said, "but sooner or later I'm going to have to go get help or at least find a rope to pull you out of here. If Gerald went back behind the building like I asked him to do, he's not likely to hear us. I'm not even sure if I can climb out of here."

"I know, I know," Heather sighed. "Just give me a few minutes to get my courage up. I know it's silly. You won't leave me down here, but I feel so trapped. My therapist says I have claustrophobia.

Jack laughed aloud. "Yeah, sure you do."

"What, you don't believe me?"

"Heather, there are few places I can think of less confined than this. If you were truly claustrophobic, you would in a big panic about right now."

"Well, I'm slightly claustrophobic."

Jack shook his head.

"I am. Just a little…"

"No," Jack said. "If you have a fear of anything, it's a fear of being alone."

"I'm not afraid of being alone."

"Good. Then I'm going to get help." He started to get up.

"No, please don't," she pleaded. "Not yet. Okay, okay, maybe you're right. Maybe I am afraid of being alone. Big deal. I bet you're not afraid of anything, are you? No, of course not. You're too much of a macho man. You don't even know what fear is, do you?"

Jack looked across to the other side of the dirt wall for a long time. "I'm afraid of going to sleep," he said somberly.

"Sleep?" She almost sneered. "Why?"

"Because when I sleep," he said laboriously, "I have nightmares."

"Everybody has nightmares."

"I have one that won't go away." He thrust his hand into the wall of dirt and began clawing an opening.

"What are you doing now?" Heather said, wearily.

"Making toe holds. It might be a way out."

"I told you before, I'm not staying down here by myself."

"You won't have to," Jack said, "I'll carry you up on my back."

Heather laughed. "You are going to carry me all the way up there? Digging little holes along the way? Yeah, and when I land, I'll be sure to fall on my *good* leg this time."

"Look," Jack said, furiously, "I don't hear any great plans coming from you. Do you want to stay down here forever?"

"Gerald should be coming for us soon."

"I doubt it. Even if he does, what's going to stop him from coming down on top of us?"

Heather looked nervously up to the opening. "Keep digging."

"I can't believe I was stupid enough to fall for this," Jack said, grunting.

"Well, they should put danger signs around something like this. What idiots dig a giant hole and then cover it up with rotted wood?"

"What idiots trespass on private property looking for more idiots? Besides, that's not what I'm talking about. I'm talking about this whole scam."

Heather tried to reposition herself but was halted by the pain. "What scam?"

"Oh, come on. Even you can't be that dense. Ten thousand dollars just to live with some people for a week. I should have smelled a rat as soon as I read it. I must be getting old."

"What are you talking about, Jack?"

Jack stopped digging and turned to her. "If it sounds too good to be true, it usually is. We fell for it hook, line, and sinker. There's no ten thousand dollars. There's no mysterious experiment. There's only a bunch of gullible fools and one kleptomaniac woman who thinks she's a member of Special Forces."

"Are you saying she lured us here just to steal from us?"

"That's exactly what I'm saying." He started digging again.

Heather shook her head. "No, that doesn't make any sense. If she were going to lure anybody, wouldn't it be people with money? And why the silly rule about not leaving the house? Seems to me, she would want us to leave so she could rob us while we were gone."

"I don't know," Jack admitted, "I haven't figured that out yet. Who knows what goes on in that deranged head of hers."

Heather looked down as if she were going to cry. "No ten thousand dollars? I really needed that money!"

"Money isn't everything."

"Maybe not, but it sure would help with some bills."

"Yeah," Jack reflected with a sigh, "I was going to find me a nice office to work out of."

"An office?" Heather asked doubtfully. "What do you do, anyway?"

"I'm a private investigator."

Heather raised an eyebrow. "Private investigator," she said, letting the words roll slowly off her tongue as if they were new to her. "I should have guessed. It makes sense now."

Jack was standing up now, digging out little holes above his head. He turned again, his anger swelling. "And just what do you mean by that?"

"I mean it makes sense to me now," she said defensively, "you always seem to be figuring things out in your head. You were the only one who noticed that the army woman went through our stuff. You seemed to know about John's real estate con. I was just saying that you have a good mind for that type of work, that's all."

"Oh," he said, changing his tone. "I'll take that as a compliment." He slid down to the ground again and rested.

"Don't let it go to your head, there's plenty of room left for improvement for you."

Jack rubbed his sweaty forehead. "Oh yeah? Like what?"

"You really don't want me to start that list, do you?"

"Just name one."

"Well...like that nasty smoking habit of yours."

Jack nodded in agreement. Then he promptly took out a cigarette, lit it and puffed some smoke in her direction. "You're right. They'll probably kill me eventually."

Heather shook her head in disgust and coughed from the smoke. Jack smiled in the half-light and took another drag. They were quiet for a time and then Heather broke the silence. "Tell me about your nightmare," she said, carefully.

Jack remained quiet for a time and then looked distant as if peeling back layers of memories. "I used to be a cop," he said at last.

"Wow, Jack, you're full of surprises," Heather said.

He ignored her and continued his story. "I'd been with the force for over ten years. One night, my partner and I were cruising. It was pretty late and our shift was nearly over. Then we got this call from dispatch...a robbery in progress. I can still remember the look on Baker's face.

Baker was my partner. When he looked at me, it was kind of a worried expression. But there was also some expectation there, some excitement. You have to understand, being a cop isn't like all those TV shows. You don't go out every time and end up in a shooting match with drug dealers or some 120 mile per hour car chase. I knew some guys that had twenty years in the force and never drew their weapon. I had never drawn mine."

He crushed out what remained of his cigarette and fumbled for another one. He lit the last one in the pack and crumpled the empty carton before continuing. "Most nights were pretty boring. The most excitement we saw was on domestic calls. People get drunk, they get violent. Pretty soon, they want to fight the whole world. Anyway, we got this robbery call. It was a convenience store out on the edge of town. I knew we were pretty close and would probably get there first. There's a kind of…adrenaline rush you get when you know you're going into that kind of situation. I mean, it's not the kind of excitement you might think. Most people seem to think it's all gung-ho and 'let's go get the bastards'. It's not. It's an excitement that puts you on edge. You wonder how it's gonna go down. You think that if you make one wrong move, it might make all the difference in the world and you or your partner or both could end up dead.

"We got there right at the end. The suspect was fleeing on foot. The store clerk ran out front and was waving his arms in the direction the man went. At this point, I was glad nobody was hurt. This could mean that the clerk was held up with a knife or something other than a gun. We had to assume he had a gun, though, so we would be prepared for the worst. In any case, we didn't have time to ask questions. The suspect was getting away. Baker swung the car through the parking lot and down the edge of the road. We had him in our headlights for a few seconds and then he darted to the left into the woods."

***

"Christ," Baker said, "he's going into the park. If he gets too far, we may never find him." He slammed on the brakes, bringing the police cruiser to a skidding halt. Officer Jack Eastman was shooting words into the radio. He informed dispatch the last known location of the suspect and that they were now taking up pursuit on foot. He knew there would be others on the way for backup, but there was no time to wait for them. The two officers headed into the park, their flashlight beams dancing wildly on trees and shrubs, making a sudden threat out of every moving shadow.

"Split off," Baker said, sounding as if he were already out of breath. "I'll curve around left, you take the right."

Jack agreed and ran along his new path, aware of his partner's light moving away with the changing distance. He tried to steady his own light, quickly scanning to cover the greatest area and attempting to be as thorough as possible. The further he went, the more the possibility of danger weighed upon his mind. With the suspect out of sight, he could be anywhere, hiding behind a tree or waiting ahead to take them out. As he ran, he became aware of his own heavy breathing and he could feel his heart pounding in his chest.

Baker's flashlight was now out of site and Jack felt alone in the woods. In a sudden, unexplained fear, he imagined plowing right into the suspect and his waiting knife. Just then, his leg came into contact with something hard and it sent him flying down into the dirt. He rolled around quickly and flashed his light at the would-be assailant. It was a tree stump. Then he became vividly aware of the pain radiating from his shin. But he was distracted by a voice in the distance. Realizing Baker was yelling, he quickly got up and limped painfully in the direction of the voice. His progress seemed to be unbelievably slow and he cursed under his breath.

In a small clearing, Baker held his gun and flashlight on a figure laying face down on the ground. "Move your hands slowly out where I can see them," Baker commanded.

Except for some violent shivering, the figure didn't move. Baker was breathing heavy and his voice sounded out the desperation of the situation. "I'm not going to tell you again. Put your hands behind your head."

But the figure did not put his hands behind his head. Instead, he pushed himself slowly up, his back to the police officer. He turned slowly to face his capturer, simultaneously moving his hands upward. There was a gun in one of his hands.

Two ear-splitting shots rang out. Two bloodstained holes appeared from nowhere in the suspect's chest. "No," Baker cried, his head jerking back in shock. He ran to the falling, bleeding man. The shots were clean and deadly.

It was like slow motion to Jack now. Still holding his aimed gun, he moved slowly to where his partner searched frantically for a way to keep the man from dying. Jack saw it all in a blur. Baker looked up at him with a helpless expression he would never forget. He slowly walked around and glanced over at the suspect's weapon that had fallen to the ground. It was a plastic toy pistol.

***

Jack's head was resting on his knees now. He pushed his unfinished cigarette into the ground, crushing it into several broken pieces.

"Jack..." Heather began, sympathetically.

"It was a sixteen-year-old kid," Jack said, looking up. His eyes were glassy and he looked suddenly older. "Sixteen years old. Do you know what I was doing when I was sixteen? I was trying to fix up an old worn-down car so I could start driving when I got my license. I was a high-school hero on our football team. I had my whole life in front of me and I knew it all. I was invincible just like any other teenager. But nobody can ever get through to you at that age, you know? Nobody can make you realize that you're not invincible. Maybe if somebody could have told this kid..."

He trailed off and pushed his hair back. Heather looked at him as if seeing him for the first time. There was someone there underneath the hard surface. Someone who wasn't always in control. There was part of a man there that needed the help of a friend just like anybody else.

"It wasn't your fault, Jack," Heather said softly.

"No," Jack said, quietly, "it wasn't. They went out of their way to prove it, too. They went so far as to re-enact the entire situation under the same lighting conditions. The final report told in great detail how, from my point of view, it looked as if the kid was turning a gun on my partner."

"So you were cleared," Heather said.

"I turned in my badge that night," Jack said. "After the final report came out, the chief was so kind as to call me up and give me the good news. I was cleared. What he really meant was that the department was cleared. There would be no formal charges to stain the department's reputation. But he said everything was okay and to come back to work. They had made it okay that I shot a sixteen-year-old kid in the line of duty."

"But it wasn't okay with you, was it?"

"No. I never went back."

"But you keep looking back," Heather said carefully. "You can't let it go."

"No," Jack admitted. "Not yet. I will someday, I think. But not yet."

"I know you will," Heather said, reassuringly. "It just takes time."

"Yeah, a lot of it," Jack said. He smiled grimly at her. "Thanks for listening. It felt good to talk about it." He was returning to his old self now, looking up at the round opening. He stood up again, grimacing from a pain that shot up his back. "Let's get out of this hell hole," he said.

CHAPTER NINETEEN

John sighed and closed another book. He sat in the library at a study table buried with stacks of reference books. "It's hopeless," he said and put his head down on the table.

Gail peered over a homes and garden magazine at her distraught husband. She said, "I'm sorry, dear. You tried your best."

John looked up at her. His face wore a mixed expression of fatigue and irritation. "It's just so frustrating," he told her. "This is the kind of research I'm good at. It's what I do. If it weren't for this antiquated town, I would have found the information in no time. If I had my computer..."

Gail put a finger to her lips. "Dear, perhaps the computer they have here can help you find what we're looking for."

John blinked. "What do you mean? What computer?"

"I saw one at the other end of the library. I guess it's for kids doing research on the Internet."

Her husband leaned towards her from across the table. "They have a computer here with access to the Internet and you didn't tell me?"

"Well," she explained, "I didn't know you could make use of it.

John groaned and got up. "Show me where this computer you speak of is. I must say, I am doubtful they have even heard of computers in this town, let alone have one hooked up to the outside world."

Gail led him into the back of the library where a lone computer contrasted the surrounding books and old microfilm machines. On their approach, the electronic station appeared to be unoccupied, but as they drew closer and could see over the monitor, a small girl came into view. She seemed to be no more than five or six years old. She looked up at them with oversized bifocal glasses. She considered the strange, older faces for a moment and returned to her work.

John and Gail smiled at each other, seeing how precious the little girl was. John bent down and smiled at her. "Whatcha doing?"

"Re-serts," the girl said, her eyes glued to the screen.

"Oh. Well, that's pretty important stuff. I have to do some research too. Do you think I could use the computer now?"

Her little legs swung freely in the big chair she was sitting in. "Nope," she said, flatly.

"Ah, c'mon," John coaxed, "I promise I won't use it for very long. Then you can get back to your studies."

The girl turned to him momentarily and rolled her magnified eyes upward. "I've got to be done wif dis today. My report's gonna be due tomorrow."

"Well, you know," John said, his impatience growing, "there's a lot of information that you can find in all these books in here. Why don't you go look up the information you need in them?"

The little girl tapped the keyboard in sync with her words. "Why - don't - you?"

John stood up again. "Now see here, you little -"

Gail grabbed him by the arm and pulled him back to a nearby bookshelf. "You're not going to get anywhere by yelling at her."

"Well, what am I supposed to do?" John asked, exasperated. "She thinks the thing is her own private toy."

"Let me handle this," she said and walked back to where

the little girl was studying the screen. Pretending to peer excitedly out of the nearby window, she said, "Oh my, I do believe I see the ice cream truck coming."

The girl shook her head slowly. "Not gonna work," she said.

"Oh, for goodness sakes," Gail said, reaching into her pocket. She squatted down, eye level with the girl and held up a crumpled five-dollar bill. She said, "Give us ten minutes."

The girl considered the money, appearing cross-eyed as she looked down her nose at it. She grabbed the bill and started to leave, but turned back to Gail. "Better be off it when I get back." Then she was gone.

Gail sighed and motioned for her husband to come out of his hiding. "Get to work. We don't have much time."

***

"Heather, you're choking me," Jack gasped. He was three-quarters of the way up the hole and Heather clung to him like a parasite as he tried to dig out his next foothold.

"Well, I'm sorry Jack, but this was your crazy idea, not mine."

"Just quit choking me…I can't breathe."

"I'm not choking you," Heather said. "If I were choking you, you would know it. I can't loosen my grip, either, so don't even ask. If I loosen my grip, I'll fall and break my other leg. Do you want that to happen?"

At this point, Jack felt like pulling her arms apart and letting her fall like so much excess baggage. He said sharply, "If you don't loosen your grip, I'm going to lose consciousness, we're going to fall again and you will have 190 pounds of dead weight falling on top of you. Do you want *that* to happen?"

Heather groaned. "Why do you always have to be so difficult?" She loosened her grip around his neck and, to make up for it, quickly dug her long nails into his chest.

Jack grimaced as he pulled them up one more step. He

was very close to reaching the top of the hole now. "If you make it out of here alive, you'll be lucky," he said.

"Jack, you mean if 'we' make it out of here alive, right? Jack?"

***

Gerald watched intently as Paul edged ever closer. The big man was standing in the middle of the building now, surveying all the surrounding nooks and crannies that Kola could be hiding in. "I can wait all day, woman," he said. His voice boomed in the confines of the large building. "Yer gonna have to come out sooner or later."

Gerald's eyes widened as he saw a flash of movement from the large funnel. It was the army women. She had somehow made her way to the top of the funnel and was moving dangerously close to the edge. She crouched down in a jumping position. Gerald felt like shouting to warn Paul, but then thought better of it. He saw visions of Paul shooting the women as she flew through the air. His mind raced with indecision. What should he do?

But there was no time to make a decision. Like a trained paratrooper, she dropped from her vantage point, hitting Paul in the back and sending him tumbling to the floor. His gun was knocked free of his grasp and slid a few feet away. His assailant also hit the floor hard, but tumbled expertly and regained her footing. She moved quickly to retrieve the gun and opened the chamber, spilling the ammunition onto the floor. Then she flung the weapon as far as she could throw it. It clattered loudly, dancing over steel tracks forty feet away.

Paul was on all fours. He shook his head groggily and looked in the direction of his clattering gun. Then he looked up at Kola. His voice was hoarse when he spoke. "My pah gave me that gun. You done signed yer death warrant."

Kola stepped back and took a martial arts stance. She held her fists out in front of her and beckoned him with one of them. "Come on, big man. You want to take me on?

Give me your best shot."

"Oh," Paul said, with a fierce grin, "you're gonna get a lot more than that." He bolted upward like a raging bull and headed straight for her mid-section. Kola easily sidestepped his attack and kicked him in the rear, causing him to fall again to the hard floor.

"If that's your best..." Kola said, shaking her head. But Paul was already getting up. An angry growl arose from his throat as he charged again. Again, Kola avoided his onslaught and sent him flying out of control onto the floor. It took Paul a little longer to get up this time as he cursed under his breath. He stood up, straightened to full height and held up his fists. "All right, women. All it takes is one good hit from me. I'm gonna knock you from here to Sunday."

Kola smiled deviously and nodded her head, returning to her original stance. She walked slowly toward him, her fists held at chin level. Paul watched her with sinister eyes, waiting until she got close enough. Then he jabbed a right-handed punch intended for her jaw. Kola quickly ducked back and to the left. Paul threw another one. This time it was a left. Kola ducked right. Paul brought forth a quick blow towards her stomach, but Kola bowed her body. Frustrated, Paul brought his fists back and thought about what his next move should be. Kola took advantage of his hesitation and spun around quickly with a high kick that slammed into the side of his head. Again, Paul found himself on all fours. Kola followed up the attack with a swift kick to the stomach that was meant to send him tumbling over. She had underestimated his weight, though, and her foot merely caught his belly hard and stopped. Her momentary surprise was just enough to allow Paul to grab her outstretched leg. He grunted as he pulled it forward, sending her straight down to the floor. She winced from the pain in her backside but quickly rolled over to regain her footing. Again, she was too late. Paul held her down with his weight. Then put his massive arm around her neck and dragged her up to her knees.

"All right," he said. "Now we're gonna see what yer made of."

Kola first gasped, then tried to pull his arm away with both hands. Realizing this was futile, she immediately bit into his flesh. Paul groaned in pain, but only tightened his grip around her neck. She relinquished quickly and tried to catch her breath.

"How 'bout if I just break your neck?" Paul said angrily.

Suddenly, he felt an arm around his own neck. "Let her go, Paul," Jack said.

"What the...? Get off me, man. I'm gonna make 'er wish she was never born."

Heather came limping around to the side. "Polecat, what are you doing? Let her go. You're going to hurt her."

"That's the idea," Paul said sharply. "She done beat the tar out of me."

"Let her go," Jack demanded. "Now!"

"I ain't gonna - "

A gunshot echoed throughout the building like an exploding cannon. They all turned to see Sheriff Clay standing near the entrance with his pistol in the air. "Break it up," he shouted. "Break it up now and get your hands in the air."

CHAPTER TWENTY

Sheriff Clay walked up to the group and returned the pistol to its holster. His eyes moved suspiciously over each one of them. Jack and Heather were dirty from head to toe. Paul was still catching his breath and looked back at the Sheriff with a big black eye. Then he saw Kola and he shook his head slowly and sighed. "Put your hands down. Will somebody tell me what's going on here?"

Jack said, "That's exactly what we've been wondering, Sheriff. This woman is your sister?"

Sheriff Clay nodded his head. "Yeah, she's my sister all right."

Jack clenched his teeth. "She's the one that stole our belongings. Her and this idiot." He jabbed a finger in Paul's direction. "And don't tell me you don't know who he is because he works for his brother just down the road from your office."

The Sheriff sighed again. "Yeah, I figured it was him when you told me your story. I was just hoping it was someone else." He turned to his sister. "Kola, did you steal from these people?"

Jack looked over to the army women and muttered the new name. "Kola?"

Kola did not answer, but walked over to a nearby conveyor machine, moved some material aside and retrieved

118

her backpack. She hurled the bag at her brother's feet. "I would have given it back if this fat moron hadn't screwed everything up."

"Give me a break," Jack said, "do you really expect us to believe that?"

"My sister is not a thief," Sheriff Clay said. "What she did was wrong and she will pay for the damages, but you can believe that she wouldn't have kept your things. You went too far this time, Kola."

Heather coughed. "This time? What else as she done?"

"She specializes in 'covert operations'," the Sheriff began. Then he saw a movement beyond the group, towards the other end of the building. He called out, "You, hiding behind the forklift. Come out of there."

Presently, two raised hands came into view followed by Gerald's thin figure. "I, uh…"

"Come on, Gerald," Jack said, "join the crowd."

The Sheriff shook his head again. "As I was saying. My sister, as you may have noticed, takes her military training a little too far. She's due back to her unit soon. Isn't that right, Kola?"

Heather looked at her incredulously. "The military? But how did you know about us meeting together and everything?"

"She didn't," Jack said. "I think when she broke the back door in, she wasn't expecting to find anybody home. From what I told her, she must have ascertained that the rest of us didn't know each other or who was going to show up, so she invited herself. But what I don't understand- " he turned to Kola's direction – "is how you found out so much about it. Were you hiding in the bushes with Paul?"

Kola looked at him with a stern face and said nothing. Gerald, finally lowering his arms as he joined the group and said, "She went through all our stuff, right? I had a copy of the invitation letter in my bag."

"Of course," Jack said with a smirk. "You just played right in, making yourself out to be one of the guests. But what the hell did you think you would accomplish by stealing from us and cutting our fuel lines?"

"So that was your mission objective this time?" Sheriff Clay asked her. "Get in, retrieve the valuables and get out, leaving the enemy helpless to pursue?"

Jack winced. "Mission objective? What is she, Special Forces?"

"That's what she likes to think she is," Sheriff Clay said.

"You've already told them too much," Kola said suddenly.

"Kola 'works' in Grander county mental hospital," Sheriff Clay continued. "She's uh…an undercover operative there."

"I see," Jack said slowly.

"You're blowing my cover," Kola said tightly.

"Don't worry, Kola," Sheriff Clay said. "I'll make sure these people don't say anything." He moved to one side with Jack and spoke quietly. "I'm really sorry about this. This is the second time she's broken out. The doctors tell me they are real close to making a breakthrough and this will probably be a big setback for her."

"What happened to her?" Jack asked.

"I don't know. Something happened in the military during her training. There's an open investigation on it, but whatever happened, it really messed her up."

"I'm sorry to hear that," Jack said. "I'm sure in light of this, none of us will press charges. But sheriff, I have to say, I really thought she was the one that lured us to the house. So, if it wasn't her, then who?"

"I'm afraid I can't help you there. As long as you aren't victims of fraud or some other crime, there is no reason for me to investigate. I would suggest you pack up your things and go back home."

"Well, I'm fine with that," Jack said, looking over in Kola's direction. "But unfortunately, somebody cut our fuel lines."

The Sheriff nodded and turned to the others. "That's one thing I think I can help you with. Paul is going to accompany me to his brother's garage where we will arrange for the beginning of his community service."

Paul squinted at the Sheriff. "Community service? That's just another way of saying that you want me to work fer free. I ain't gonna do that. Besides, yer sister's the one who did the damage."

"My sister has to go back to her 'headquarters', the Sheriff said. "But you have a choice. You can either go to jail or you can work weekdays and go hunting on the weekend. You won't do much hunting from a jail cell."

Sheriff Clay picked up the backpack and handed it to Jack. He looked at Heather. Her hair was unkempt, her face was spotted with dirty patches and she stood barefoot on one leg, leaning on Jack for support. Her expression of dazed futility was quite different from that of the person who had introduced herself earlier that day. "Are you all right, ma'am?" he asked.

"I just want to leave this horrid place," she said.

"That sounds like a good idea to me," Sheriff Clay said. "Let's all get out of here before I have to explain to the mining company why we're all trespassing."

CHAPTER TWENTY-ONE

The puke-green VW sputtered its way back towards the summer home, having picked up John and Gail along the way. "Oh my," Gail was saying, "and I thought we had an adventure. It must have been absolutely dreadful in that hole."

Heather, who was crammed in the bug's front passenger seat, held her leg and winced with pain. "You have no idea," she said.

"Yeah, we had a great time," Jack said. "So, you were telling us what you found out about the owners of the house."

"Yes, it's quite interesting," John said. "I was able to track it down to the Bureau of Forestry. It would seem that the land the house is on has been selected to be cleared in the near future. At least, that's what I thought. Then I found a document where a previous private owner had found a loophole in the previous sale of the property and was contesting the legitimacy of the ownership. It just got worse from there, I'm afraid. Somehow, there is another government agency involved that revoked all ownership of the property and assigned it to an unknown entity. The whole paper trail ends up where it begins. I've never seen anything like it. I may have been able to make some sense of it given time, but it was like running into a brick wall everywhere I turned. Besides, my ten minutes was up."

"Ten minutes?" Jack asked.

"It's a long story," Gail said.

At last, the large house came into view as they traveled the final stretch. The cloud of dust that followed them was thrown forth by the wind and overtook the car as Gerald slowed. Suddenly, a wall came into view through the dust and Gerald hit the brakes just in time.

"Uh, sorry for the quick stop," Gerald said. "It's a good thing your truck is down the road, Jack. I would have hit it that time for sure."

Heather turned sharply to Jack, her eyes narrow. Jack shrugged his shoulders and grinned.

They all piled out of the car and stood for a moment as the dust settled. Heather thought about her car and wondered that perhaps the garage could fix her hood for free as well. As the air cleared she looked towards her car, but something didn't seem right. She blinked. The dust was completely gone now, but it didn't look right. It looked as if her windows were smashed in, her taillights busted out and numerous dents had plagued her car. Her mouth dropped and she hobbled around the bug towards what was left of her car, making little gasping noises as she went.

The rest of them could only look on in disbelief as Heather reached her battered vehicle and stretched her arms over the top of her car. "My beautiful car," she sobbed. "Who would do something like this?"

Jack was eyeing the windows of the house now. "Vandals would be my guess." He went over to Heather and pulled her gently away, helping her walk. She was still pointing at the car as if not everybody had seen the full magnitude of what happened to it.

They walked into the doorway and stopped short. The walls were tattered with holes and covered with orange spray paint. The stairway banister was destroyed with only a few random poles sticking up like oversized toothpicks. The windows were smashed as well as the lamps and tables. Chairs were overturned and upholstery ripped. They looked down to see splinters of wood and trash floating across a flooded floor.

Gerald squinted in amazement. "Boy, the owners are gonna be pissed."

"Yes," John said in a low voice. "Whoever they are."

Jack wrinkled his nose. "God, what is that stench."

It was then that they looked down and saw the head of a dear floating by. Heather buckled and began making heaving sounds. Jack grabbed her and they all moved quickly back outside where they settled against the wall of the house. Heather broke away from Jack and hobbled over behind Gerald's car where she immediately got sick.

Jack shook his head. "Whatever this experiment was supposed to prove, this wasn't part of the deal. No amount of money is worth going through this."

"A-men," John said. Gail walked over to Heather and helped her to sit in the VW. Heather looked dismally up only to see the remains of her car in the view. Then she put her head back down.

Jack turned to Gerald and John. "Let's see if we can gather our belongings if we have any left worth keeping. The sooner we get out of here, the better."

Gerald felt something rubbing against his legs and looked down to find his feline friend. "Kitty!" He reached down and picked up the cat. It purred loudly as he petted it."

"It would appear," John said, indicating the dwelling, "that your friend is in dire need of a new home. I don't think anyone would object."

"Oh, wow," Gerald said, "do you really think so? I'll take real good care of it."

"I'm sure it would be much better than leaving it here," Jack agreed.

***

The last bag was added to the pile of luggage that now sat on the ground just outside the house. The group of suitcases mirrored their owners, appearing as a montage of misfits that would soon disband, but unsure of the direction.

Gerald, sensing the finality of the moment, straightened himself nervously and addressed the group. "This is goodbye, isn't it? I mean, it's hard for me to believe I won't ever see any of you again. I mean, after you get your cars fixed and head out of town."

Heather looked up with a bittersweet smile. "You never know, Gerald. Anything can happen."

"We can keep in touch," Gail added. "Send a letter from time to time so we can keep up to date on things."

Gerald frowned. "That's what people always say. But they never do. I don't know how all of you feel, but I know I'm going to miss you guys."

The awkward moment was interrupted by the sound of an approaching vehicle. Off in the distance, dust billowed in cloud layers behind it.

"It better be a tow truck," Jack said. But as they watched, the vehicle took on the form of a small white and blue jeep. It was a mail truck.

"This place doesn't even have a mailbox," Gerald said. "What is he doing coming out here?"

"The house is remote," Jack said. "Maybe he only delivers once a week or something."

"It will be interesting to see what name is on the address," John commented.

The jeep pulled up, ushering in a fresh wave of dust and came to a halt. A tall man in a blue uniform got out with a big bulging envelope under his arm. He walked up and slowed when he saw the tattered group. Then he continued up to Jack, who was the closest. His mirrored sunglasses reflected a distorted house. "Howdy," he said as he held out the envelope.

Jack nodded to the man. "Uh…we don't exactly live here."

"Doesn't matter," the mailman said. "It's addressed to postal patron. That means anybody can get it. Probably junk mail."

Jack took the envelope. "And you drove all the way out

here to deliver it."

The mailman started back to his truck. "Just doing my job, that's all." He started the vehicle and turned it around, heading back down the dirt road.

Jack held up the package and called out, "Hey, wait a minute! Hey!" But the truck did not stop. He watched the jeep as it disappeared in a dust cloud. Jack sighed and looked down at the package. Then he looked around at the others who had walked up to inspect the curious delivery.

Heather hobbled closer and coughed. "Go ahead and open it, Jack. Perhaps we've won sweepstakes or something."

"Yeah," Gerald said, "because we are so lucky."

Jack fumbled with the little fastener on the envelope, then grew impatient with it and tore the top open. Inside, he found several smaller envelopes. He pulled one out. It was plain white with a single typewritten name on the front. Jack read it aloud: "Gerald."

"What? Nobody knows I'm here," Gerald said.

"Evidently, someone does," Jack said and handed him the envelope. He retrieved another one. "John & Gail," Jack said, handing them an envelope.

"What is it?" John asked.

Jack pulled out another one and inspected the name. "Miss Heather, I think this one belongs to you," he said as he gave her an envelope. He pulled out the last one. "And one for me."

Gerald began stuttering uncontrollably as he studied the contents of his letter. "Uh--uh--oh man! Ten thousand dollars and 'an extra ten thousand for the trouble'. I have a check for twenty thousand dollars!"

"My word," John said, opening his own envelope, "he's right. It's cold, hard cash! Twenty thousand for each of us!"

They turned to Heather, whose eyes were getting as big as golf balls. She looked up as if in shock.

"Well, what is it?" Jack asked. "What did you get?"

"It says ten thousand," she said slowly, "and thirty thousand for damages. I have forty thousand dollars."

"Wow!" Gerald exclaimed.

Jack quickly opened his envelope. "Twenty thousand dollars. I can't believe it. We actually got the money!"

They all jumped in excitement and celebration and Gerald started doing the twist, singing, "My bug's gonna be like brand new!"

John turned to his wife and gave her a big kiss. He said, "And you didn't think this trip would be worthwhile." She just smiled and whacked her husband with the envelope.

Jack looked at his check to see who the benefactor was. The top left simply said: 'The McAllister Group'. He thought he might do a little investigation on it later, but he had a hunch it would probably end in a dead-end search.

After the excitement died down, the group was again met with a sort of uncomfortable silence. John Forest finished loading his and his wife's luggage into the VW.

"We'll be in town until the car is fixed," he said. "So, we will probably see you around until then."

"Yeah," Jack agreed. "Hey, maybe we can grab some dinner together later at Betsy's diner."

"A splendid idea, Jack," John said, as he and his wife piled into the VW.

Gerald got in behind the wheel and said, "I'll be back in about an hour and give you a ride into town, Heather. I'm not sure if we can fit all your luggage in here, but we'll try."

"Oh, thanks, Gerald, but no need to come all the way back up here," she said. "I will ride into town with Jack when the tow truck gets here."

Jack raised his eyebrows at this. Then Gerald started up the bug, waved goodbye and they drove off, once more creating a small dust storm as the car went down the road.

"You're going to ride in a tow-truck?" Jack said.

"I've been roughing it all week, Jack. What's one more bad experience?"

"Is that how you see everything that happened? A bad experience?"

"Well, I did meet some interesting people, that's for sure," she said. "But my car is totaled, I have a hurt leg and my favorite shoes are ruined, no thanks to you I might add."

Jack crossed his arms. "Still," he said, "I think you came out ahead on this deal. I don't think your car was worth quite that much."

"You're right, it wasn't." She laughed. "But I'm not complaining."

"That's a first," Jack said, smiling.

"You know what, Jack? I'm going to let that little remark go because you are going to pay me back."

"Pay you back?"

"That's right. There is no fixing my car, so I'm going to need a ride back home. I figure once your truck is fixed, we can find a real town and you can buy me a very expensive dinner in a very expensive restaurant."

Jack raised his eyebrows again. "Is that what you figure?"

"Yes, Jack, that's what I figure. You wouldn't argue with me, would you?"

"Who, me?" Jack said, smiling. Then he added, sarcastically, "I would never dream of doing that."

THE END